'I spoke to my lawyer again today, about giving you custody of the children, and he said again it would be better if you were married. Is there anyone, Dierdre, whom you want to marry?'

'Well,' she began, blushing deeply, glad that Fiona could not see her, 'there is a doctor at the hospital—the kids have met him—whom I really like. He's divorced, and unfortunately marriage isn't a top priority for him. He's told me that he doesn't trust love. Those were his words.'

'Well, dear, you will have to show him otherwise,' Fiona said, as though it was the easiest thing in the world.

Rebecca Lang trained to be a State Registered Nurse in Kent, England, where she was born. Her main focus of interest became operating theatre work, and she gained extensive experience in all types of surgery on both sides of the Atlantic. Now living in Toronto, Canada, she is married to a Canadian pathologist and has three children. When not writing, Rebecca enjoys gardening, reading, theatre, exploring new places, and anything to do with the study of people.

Recent titles by the same author:

NURSE ON ASSIGNMENT

THE SURGEON'S CONVENIENT FIANCÉE

BY
REBECCA LANG

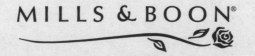

First published in Great Britain 2006
Harlequin Mills & Boon Limited,
Eton House, 18-24 Paradise Road, Richmond, Surrey TW9 1SR

© Rebecca Lang 2006

ISBN 0 263 84726 8

Set in Times Roman 10½ on 12½ pt.
03-0406-56918

Printed and bound in Spain
by Litografia Rosés, S.A., Barcelona

CHAPTER ONE

DEIRDRE first understood that something was wrong when she failed to get off the bus at her customary stop.

It was odd, really, because that was definitely the right stop, she thought as the bus started up again after letting someone off.

As she watched, unable to move, she felt as though her legs were two sacks filled with heavy stones that she could not possibly lift to put one foot in front of the other. Her whole body had become a heavy, leaden thing that refused to obey her internal command. She could not understand it at first, this stubborn refusal.

She should have got off there, the nearest stop to the house, because she had four heavy plastic bags of groceries to carry. There they were beside her on the seat. Of course they were hers, she knew that in a distant sort of way because she remembered having walked around a supermarket very recently, pushing the usual metal cart. The memory of that was very clear in her mind.

As the bus jerked forward she felt slightly sick, the feeling reminding her that she had forgotten to have any sort of lunch, and now it was the end of the afternoon. There was so much on her mind these days that she even forgot to eat. No doubt her blood sugar was low, she speculated, her nursing training coming to the fore.

Too late now to get off the bus. It was picking up speed, bowling along towards the next stop, which was two blocks away. Deirdre wondered vaguely, with a sense of fear, whether she was going mad. Coupled with her odd inertia was a reluctance to look at her wristwatch. She wanted time to be still for a while so that she could just sit and not have to do anything, or think about anything in particular. In a vague way she understood that.

Slowly, reluctantly, she gathered up the plastic bags that were bulging with groceries and got off the bus when it came to a halt at the next stop. Momentarily she felt lost, although she knew where she was—of course she did.

'What now?' she said aloud, causing an elderly man near her to look at her sharply, and then away again quickly.

As she began to walk back the way she had come, it was as though she were split into two people—one felt lost and vulnerable, the other distanced from that self, logical, sensible, almost like a mother figure who was taking care of the other half. By getting off the bus two blocks further on, she was giving herself time to think, to distance herself.

Jerry would be back in town that evening. She ought to be pleased at that, as it meant that she could return to her own home and would not have to sleep in Jerry's house to be with the children. Instead, she felt an odd feeling of panic, and she did not really want to leave them with him...

It was a crisp November day, quite cold, beginning to get gloomy now. There were few people about in this part of the city, which bordered on a residential area. As she walked, she realized that she had not been this way for a very long time. So long, in fact, that she had almost forgotten about the existence of the hospital in the centre of the first city block that she had to pass, the Stanton Memorial Hospital. It was a relatively small hospital, affiliated to a large teaching hospital downtown, and one that had escaped the cost-cutting closures of some other small hospitals in recent years.

Beyond that, Deirdre knew little about the hospital—having worked in the large teaching hospital herself before the budget cuts—except that it took interns and some residents-in-training on a rotating basis from the bigger hospital. Strange, really, she thought now that she, a nurse, who lived so close to the hospital, should know so little about it, especially when she had so desperately wanted to find another job in a hospital after she had been laid off. But then, of course, she had taken the job with Jerry, looking after the children. It had been a stopgap job, which had somehow taken over her whole life so that she had stopped looking for jobs in nursing.

As she came level with the hospital she could see that there was a noticeboard, enclosed in glass, like a cupboard, set in the garden facing the street, next to the sidewalk and between the curving entrance and exit driveways. With the heavy bags at her feet, glad of a rest, she looked at it. Inside the locked case were a variety of notices pertaining to hospital business as it related to the general public. Then she saw the notice headed 'Employment Opportunities' and her heart quickened with interest.

'But you're not free,' the persistent voice inside her head reminded her, the one that chattered a lot. Nonetheless, her eyes moved down the list until she came to 'Operating Room Nurses'. There were vacancies for full-time and part-time registered nurses in the operating suite. A refresher course would be nice, because she felt that her skills were rusty. No doubt there would be a two- to three-week orientation period.

Deirdre wrote down the telephone number of the human resources department, to which one had to apply for a job. The act of doing so only served to highlight her problem of not being free. How wonderful it would be to go to work in the morning, work a set number of hours, then go home again, to her own home. Yet it seemed that fate had somehow directed her here. Sometimes she believed in that kind of fate—serendipity, or whatever it was called.

She began to plod forward again, burdened with the bags. Her mind seemed to be all over the place, searching this way and that for a way out of her dilemma. A light rain had begun to fall, and the early evening gloom was deepening prematurely. If only she didn't love the children so much. Because she loved them, she felt trapped, was trapped. It wasn't as though Jerry and his mother-in-law paid her a decent salary, anywhere near what she was worth. No doubt if he had had his way, he would not have paid her anything at all after a while, out of his own pocket, for the work that she did to benefit him and his house. He would have coerced her into a relationship and said to her, 'We're as good as married.' Heaven knew, he had tried. She hadn't wanted that: she did not love him and never would. As it was, she found him more or less repulsive. She had known from the beginning that most of the money for her salary came from the children's maternal grandmother.

She had been twenty-three when she had gone to work for him and the grandmother, so desperate for work—an idealistic twenty-three, if not totally naïve. 'I hate him,' she said aloud. 'I wish he would disappear off the face of the earth.' Quickly she looked behind her to see if anyone was within earshot. These days she had taken to talking to herself, a sign of loneliness, perhaps…or worse. There was no one around.

Deirdre stepped off the kerb, looking straight ahead, to cross the exit driveway of the hospital. There was a screech of brakes and she screamed as a large dark blue car came to a halt a few inches away from her. Confused and shocked, she registered too late that she had stepped off the kerb without looking, even though the car had its headlights on.

One of the plastic bags slipped from her grasp and she watched two tins roll away from her across the driveway and various packages spill out at her feet. A man got out of the driver's seat.

'Are you all right?' he said. He sounded both angry and concerned. He had every right to be angry, Deirdre thought as she stared back at him in shock, knowing how close she had come to being an accident case. She would have seen the inside of an operating room all right, but not in the way she had envisioned. A wave of despair came over her as she looked back at him, and she could only nod, not being able to find a voice. In fact, to her mortification, she wanted to burst out crying, as though a breaking point had been reached, that this was the thing that her refusal to get off the bus had been leading up to; it was as if this thing was giving her permission to cry. For a few seconds she fully understood what the term 'accident prone' really meant. Most likely it was a cry for help.

Jerry was often angry these days, the thought came to her; angry at everyone and everything, it seemed.

The man who had got out of the car came up closer to her. He was tall, slim, very good looking and sophisticated in appearance, quite young, probably a doctor, she thought. 'Are you all right?' he said again, sounding more concerned this time. He had a nice voice, deep and somehow gentle, even though he was frowning at her as though he thought she was the greatest klutz in the world, maybe someone who had a death wish.

'I'm all right,' she said, looking at him in horror, managing to find her voice. 'I…I'm sorry. I guess I stepped off the kerb without looking.'

'You did,' he said curtly. Deirdre saw that he wore a fine black cashmere turtleneck sweater under a loose-fitting soft leather jacket in a very dark brown colour that looked very, very expensive and blended perfectly with his dark grey, beautifully tailored trousers and black Oxford shoes. In spite of her acute distress, she took all this in, as though her perceptions were heightened by a sudden surge of adrenaline. He was clean-cut, with short dark hair, a pale skin and blue-grey eyes. His firm mouth and square jaw hinted to her that he was not a man to trifle with. There was certainly an air of authority about him. 'Are you in the habit of not looking where you're going?'

'No.' The word came out in a whisper. 'Sorry.' Then, to her embarrassment, tears began to run down her face, out of her control. Vaguely, she looked around her at the spilled shopping.

The sight of the tears galvanized the man into action and he took her elbow. 'Stand back on the kerb,' he said authoritatively, drawing her back. 'You've had a shock. Don't worry about your shopping, I'll pick it up.'

Standing safely on the sidewalk, she watched him chase the errant tins that had rolled to the other side of the driveway, then looked on while he picked up her other groceries.

'I'm a doctor in this hospital,' he said. 'Let me drive you home. Do you live around here?'

'Yes, not too far away,' she said, feeling infinitely weary, grateful for his suggestion yet embarrassed that he had to offer. 'Thank you.' Surreptitiously she wiped the tears off her cheeks with the back of her hand.

He placed her bags at her feet, then reached into an inside pocket for a card, which he handed to her. 'No doubt you were told by your mother not to get into a car with a strange man,' he said, smiling slightly for the first time, his tone softening. 'Very good advice.'

Deirdre glanced down at the card, blinking hard, trying to read the small print when her eyes were swimming with tears. There was a name, with a string of professional letters behind it. She took in none of it. He then fished in the outside pocket of his jacket and produced a laminated card which had a photograph on it.

'Here's my hospital ID,' he said. It showed the head and shoulders of the man in front of her, dressed in what she recognized as the top of a dark green scrub suit. By the light from the headlights of his car she could just make it out.

'Yes…I can see it's you,' she said, still not being able to read the name in the growing darkness. Also, she felt strangely distanced from the scene in which she was taking part, as though it had nothing to do with her. A few tears continued to run down her face and drip from her chin.

The man, whose name she still did not know, picked up her bags and deposited them on the back seat of his car. 'Come on,' he said, more gently now. 'I'll drive you home.' It sounded to her that, having ascertained she was not injured, he wanted to get her home and out of his hair as quickly as possible.

In the next moment she was in the front passenger seat of his very comfortable car, sinking into the capacious soft leather seat, realizing now that she was cold. 'Thank you,' she said, once again wiping the tears away with her fingers. Tactfully, he had not asked why she was crying. No doubt he assumed it was because she had very nearly been run over. 'I live on Renfrew Street.' She pointed in the general direction.

'I know it,' he said, easing the car out into the traffic.

'I do have a car,' she said, feeling she ought to say something, 'but it's out of action.'

Renfrew Street was a quiet little backwater, several short streets away from the busier street on which the hospital was situated. It was a nice street, she had to admit that, and at first she had loved the house for many reasons, not least because it had seemed like home and because that was where the children lived. Now she felt more and more claustrophobic in it.

Jerry's dark good looks, his charm—which she had come to see was carefully cultivated and calculated—his obvious need of her to look after the children had bowled her over at first. Now it all seemed so obvious and hackneyed. What had been, and was, genuine was the need that the children had of her. Children could do much to make a house seem like a home. Now all she cared about was them…and that was the trouble.

'What number?' her companion asked as he turned his car into Renfrew Street.

'Five three six,' Deirdre said, reluctant to leave the warm cocoon of the luxury car. 'Towards the other end.'

As they moved slowly down the street, she saw Jerry getting out of his car which he had parked on the street outside the house. From another car emerged three men who were obviously with Jerry and all four of them moved towards the front door of the house, intent on their animated conversation. The house was quite large, yet with no features to distinguish it from its neighbours on either side. It was a showy yet bland house, rather like its owner. Built in the California style, covered with prefabricated stucco, it was not really appropriate for the rainy and often cool climate of British Columbia, Canada.

'Oh, no!' Deirdre whispered the words. As he so often did, Jerry had brought home some colleagues, clients or friends for drinks and dinner, without warning her in advance, expecting her to do the housekeeping and cooking bit, to provide a good dinner regardless of how much food she had in the house. That was also in spite of the fact that she had been engaged to take care of the children, to cook for them but not for him.

Gradually over time she had unwisely taken on more and more work, for which she was not adequately paid. Well, maybe now was the time to call a halt. Maybe now she was approaching her breaking point. Everyone had one, she knew that.

Instinctively, in an act of self-preservation, she slid down in the seat. 'Please,' she said to the man next to her, 'drop me off at the end of the street. I've just seen someone I don't want to meet.'

The man looked at her keenly. As well he might, she thought despairingly. He must think she was off her rocker. Doing as he was asked, he went to the end of the quiet, leafy residential street and pulled over to the kerb. It was almost dark now.

'Hadn't you better tell me what's bothering you?' he said quietly. He was looking at her with interest, as one might look at an intriguing specimen under a microscope. 'Perhaps I can help in some small way. Often it helps to be able to talk to a stranger. Why are you crying? Perhaps we could start there. I'm a surgeon at the Stanton Memorial, by the way, in case you didn't take in that card I was showing you.'

'Thank you for the ride,' she said, grateful for the semi-darkness that was penetrated inadequately by street lighting. 'I'm afraid I don't know your name. I couldn't read the card.' Of course, she didn't have to know his name, although she would like to use it to thank him. In a few moments he would be out of her life as abruptly as he had entered it.

'I'm Shay Melburne,' he said. 'And you?'

'Deirdre,' she said. 'Deirdre Warwick. Thank you, Dr Melburne, for your help.' Suddenly she was very aware of him physically in the confined space, aware of his attractiveness. With that awareness came the realization that she had lacked the company of men she found attractive, as well as any decent relationship with one, in the two and a half years that she had been in her current job.

'Deirdre of the Sorrows,' he murmured. 'Rather appropriate, I would say.'

'Yes,' she said. 'You could say that.'

'A Gaelic name…like mine,' he said thoughtfully, half-turned towards her as though he were seeing her really for the first time. 'A lovely Irish name. Deirdre was a great beauty, so legend has it.'

'So I believe…if she really existed.'

'I believe she did. Why the tears, Deirdre of the Sorrows? Not because I almost ran you over, I suspect. Perhaps it was because you were crying that you didn't look where you were going. Hmm?'

'I wasn't crying then,' she said. 'It's a long story. I really can't tell you. I don't want to bore you. And…and…I don't suppose you have the time.'

'I have the time,' he said.

'Why would you bother?' she said, not believing he could be interested in hearing her story.

'Shall we say the interest of one fellow human in another?' he said. 'No other motive. I sense that you need help. I'm not saying I can provide it, but I can listen. Perhaps you can start with why you didn't want to go into that house. I've got all the time in the world.'

Deirdre cast around in her mind for a good starting point to present to this stranger. Not wanting to go into the house seemed to her to be approaching an end point, a crisis.

'I used to be a nurse,' she blurted out, 'working in the operating rooms at University Hospital.' She named the hospital downtown in Prospect Bay, where they were now, the place that had been a stop on the way to gold-mining country in the late 1800s in British Columbia. It had started off as a one-horse town and had grown into a place large enough to be called a city, growing in fits and starts over the decades. 'I loved that job. Don't want to bore you with the ins and outs of it. Got laid off about two and a half years ago…was given a pink slip, along with a lot of other nurses. In my case, it was last hired first fired. Cost-cutting…I'm sure I don't have to tell you about that.'

'No. It's starting to go the other way,' he said.

She went on to tell him how she had to earn a living, how she was helping her parents financially because her father had been ill and her mother had stopped work to look after him, how her parents had later decided to go to Australia for a long visit to see her brother, whom they had not seen for a long time. They were still there.

'And you miss them?' he asked astutely.

'Yes…very much. Sometimes it seems that I don't have parents, that they are a figment of my imagination,' she blurted out. 'Then I feel I'm going mad.' Now she was getting somewhere.

It was easy to talk to him. He listened quietly, not moving, his eyes on her face as he was turned sideways towards her.

'To cut a long story short,' she went on, 'a social worker at the hospital told me about a man, Jerry Parks, who had two children whose mother had just died of Lou Gehrig's Disease. They needed someone to take care of them.'

'The man you didn't want to see just now?'

'Yes. I was desperate for a job, so I applied and got it.'

For a few moments there was silence in the car as she wondered what to say next.

'Do you care for him, this Jerry guy?' Dr Shay Melburne asked her quietly.

'Oh, no. I dislike him…intensely,' she said, with a vehemence that she knew must have alerted him that something had indeed happened between herself and Jerry. 'But I do love the children. That's the trouble.'

'I see,' Dr Melburne said. 'You want out, is that it? But you don't want to leave the children. You've painted yourself into a corner, as it were.'

'Yes, yes! That's it exactly. And I don't know what to do about it. Oh, God! What a mess,' Deirdre moaned, with a rush of such emotion that she knew she was going to weep again in front of this stranger who would indeed think she was mad. She put her head in her hands and leaned forward, her elbows on her knees, rocking back and forth in despair.

'I can't leave them, you see…not now they've already lost their real mother. They love me, and I love them. When I first came to look after them they were so silent, so sad. Now they're more like normal children. They trust me now and need me. I don't know what to do.' When she began to sob quietly, he pushed a handkerchief into her hand and just sat beside her. 'Sorry…sorry…to lumber you with all this. I think I'm having some sort of breakdown. I…had a peculiar mental aberration just before you almost hit me with your car. That's why I wasn't looking where I was going.'

'Tell me,' he said quietly.

'I couldn't get off a bus…just couldn't make myself…at the right place.'

'Hmm,' he said. Then he waited for her to compose herself. There was an air of calm about him, as though he did actually have all the time in the world. It felt good to have someone concentrate just on you, she thought, and to ask questions as though they were really interested in the answers.

Presently he took one of her cold hands and held it between the two of his. 'It's all right,' he said. Deirdre somehow accepted the oddity of this situation; the whole day had been odd, and it was not over yet.

He waited until she had cried herself out. 'Look,' he said, 'I'd like to take you out for a meal right now. You must be hungry, and I'm starving.'

'Oh, no, you don't have to take me for a meal,' she protested, convinced that he was offering because he felt sorry for her.

'I know I don't have to. I want to,' he said firmly. 'Can you dump those groceries without encountering friend Jerry?'

'I could leave them in the garage, off the back lane,' she said. 'That is, if Basil won't get them.' She said the last bit to herself, thinking aloud.

'Who's Basil?

'Oh…he's a rat.'

Dr Melburne laughed. Surprisingly, Deirdre felt her mood of abject misery lifting a little.

'A pet rat?'

'Oh, no. He's wild, he just lives there in the walls. I'll take a chance with the groceries. I…I should cook the supper for the children, although they can cook for themselves. But I haven't seen them since this morning…' Her voice trailed off. Quite suddenly the most important thing for her in the world was to get away from her domestic situation for a while, to have a meal with this man who, she sensed, was safe and reliable.

'How old are they?'

'Mungo's thirteen and Fleur's twelve,' she said, hearing her own voice soften as she said their names. 'And another thing. He, Jerry, is not even their real father. He's their stepfather.' There was more that she could tell him, but that was enough for now. After all, this was private family information which was not just hers to divulge.

'This gets more and more complicated,' Shay Melburne said. 'Can you phone the children? I'll take all of you out. I know just the place. Have them meet us in the back lane.'

It was such a relief, for a change, to have someone else make the decisions, decisions that were also benign and in her own interests for once. 'Thank you, it's very kind of you.' Using his handkerchief, she blotted her face. 'Let's do it.'

With Deirdre directing, Shay drove around to the back lane behind the houses, one of many that the streets in the area had at the rear of the neat rows of dwellings. After letting herself in to the back garden through the gate from the lane, she put the groceries in the garage via the side door, then, using her mobile, she called Mungo on his mobile. At this moment he should be in his room, starting on his homework.

'Wow!' he said, after she had explained. 'Are we going out to eat in the middle of the week?'

'Yes,' she said. 'Get Fleur and come out to the garage. I don't want Jerry to know. Can you get out without him seeing you?'

'Yeah, he has a bunch of guys in here for drinks as usual. They're making so much noise that I can't concentrate on my essay. He didn't even check to see if we were here,' Mungo said in an aggrieved voice.

'Leave a note for him on the kitchen table, please, saying you're out to eat,' Deirdre instructed. 'Be as fast as you can.'

'You don't want him to know we're going—right?'

'Right.'

As Deirdre waited in the drizzle for the children to appear, she knew that a corner of sorts had been turned. She was beginning to fight back. Maybe things would be easier if she just coped with the children and let Jerry fend entirely for himself, if she refused to do any work other than look after the children, which was what she had been hired for. He could fire her, perhaps, but it had been the children's grandmother who had hired her, so perhaps Jerry was not in a position to dismiss her from the job. Their mother was dead, but the maternal grandmother was very much alive. They called her Granny McGregor when referring to her in her absence, although her name was Fiona and she liked to be called by that name.

It was a complicated story, she thought now as she waited. The children's biological father had never been married to their mother, they had lived as common-law husband and wife, and he had been out of the picture for some time. That was why they had their mother's surname. As far as Deirdre could ascertain, he was in South Africa and did not even know that their mother was dead, as no one had thought to tell him. He had left shortly after the birth of Fleur.

Often Deirdre wished she had known their mother, who seemed to have been a woman of intelligence, common sense and flair, with a great love for her children. Certainly she seemed to have done everything during her long illness to ensure that they would not be homeless and destitute after she died. Deirdre sensed that the only reason Jerry remained in the picture was that he hoped to get his hands on some of the money that his wife had left in trust for her two children.

She went part way down the garden path towards the house to meet Mungo and Fleur as they came silently out of the back door. 'What's up, Dee?' Fleur said to her.

'We're being taken out to supper at a restaurant by a doctor who works at the Stanton Memorial Hospital,' she said, ad-libbing. 'He gave me a ride home.'

They accepted that, as she had hoped they would, assuming that she knew the doctor well. The last thing they needed to know was that she was approaching breaking point. 'We won't be long. I know you have to get at your homework. It just saves me having to cook.'

'Jerry will be in a rage,' Fleur said gleefully. 'He just came in with three guys for drinks. I bet they want food as well.'

'Yes, that's part of the whole idea of going out,' Deirdre said, gaining courage. 'I'm not going to cook for him any more.' The decision had sort of made itself, it seemed.

In spite of her antipathy to Jerry, she did not bad-mouth

him to the children, as she did not want that to add to their underlying insecurity. Also, doing so, she suspected, would cause them to lose respect for her, even though their own feelings for him were very mixed and mostly negative. As far as possible, she tried to be neutral, while being open about problems at the same time. She was helped by the fact that part of her salary was paid out of a trust fund that had been set up by their mother. The children's grandmother had been at pains recently to inform her of that fact. Now she clung to that knowledge. It was the grandmother who was the legal guardian of the children, even though their mother had been married to Jerry.

'Good for you, Dee,' Mungo said, fully understanding. 'They can get a take-away.'

'This is Dr…um…er…Shay Melburne,' she said, introducing him as they got into the back of the car. 'Dr Melburne, this is Mungo and Fleur McGregor.'

'Very pleased to meet you both,' the doctor said, twisting around and leaning over from the front to shake hands with them in turn.

Mungo, who had untidy dark hair and steel-rimmed glasses, and was thin and deceptively boyish, gave the doctor the once-over. 'Have you known Dee very long?' he asked in a tone which Deirdre recognized as protective, and she smiled. Perhaps he thought that she had a man friend who might take her away from them.

'It…er…seems like a very long time,' Shay said, and Deirdre looked at him sharply, detecting a note of sardonic humour in his voice. She hoped he was not regretting his impulsive invitation. As though sensing exactly what she was thinking, he smiled at her, causing her heart to feel as though it were being squeezed, and she thought again how attractive he was, especially when he smiled. How nice it was to be smiled at by an attractive man…one she had begun to like, who did not seem to have a hidden agenda where she was concerned.

Fleur was equally thin, pretty in an understated way, with her fair hair and blue eyes. She had braces on her teeth, which added to her endearingly gawky and fragile air. 'Where are we going to eat?' she asked, lisping slightly because of the braces.

'I thought I'd take you to The Joker, down by the water-front,' Shay said. 'It's vegetarian. Very good. They have great pizza.'

'Ooh!' Fleur said, impressed. 'Some of my friends have been there. They rave about it. Did you used to work with Dee when she was a nurse?'

'Regrettably, we've never worked together,' he said. 'You could just say we met in the hospital environs.'

'Just hanging out?'

'You could say that.'

'Cool,' Fleur said.

'Real cool,' Mungo said. 'She didn't tell us about you, and she's been with us for two and a half years.'

'I expect she wanted to keep me all to herself up to now,' Shay said, sounding as though he wanted to laugh. 'It was my idea that the two of you might want to go out to eat, as I invited her.'

'Way to go!' Mungo said. 'Thank you.'

As they drove away down the lane, Deirdre was aware that the two children were happy to be in secure male company, to be taken out for a meal, as the attention they got from Jerry was sporadic and cursory. The novelty of it was making them smile with anticipation. For one thing, Jerry was in business, import and export, and was away a lot. Sometimes she thought that his work was of a dubious nature, perhaps to do with money-laundering, but she kept that idea strictly to herself and did not even hint to him that she knew or cared what he did, much less to Mungo and Fleur.

Dr Melburne called ahead on his mobile phone to reserve a table for them. 'Just to make sure we won't have to wait,' he said. Deirdre, sitting silently next to him, thought what an attractive name Shay was. She had never heard it before. It seemed to suit him to perfection. Beyond that, she did not want to speculate about him too much, about his private life. For the first time in a long time, part of her was feeling human again, not just the embodiment of a role that had somehow become too much for her, in spite of her love for Mungo and Fleur. The other part of her was teetering towards the brink of something. Perhaps it was a showdown with Jerry.

Now she felt the first glimmerings of what it might be like to have a partner that one could rely on, love and be loved by. Then she pushed that thought out of her mind. No point in speculating about this very attractive man whom she would not have met in normal circumstances, the way her life was now. Out of the goodness of his heart, it seemed, he was rescuing her for a short while from the routine of her life.

The restaurant was crowded, yet a table had been reserved for them, by a window overlooking the harbour of Prospect Bay, where lights twinkled and glistened on the water. It was the sort of restaurant where you could feel private, even though most of the tables were taken, the tables separated by tall potted plants.

Within a very short time Fleur and Mungo had perused the menu and chosen unusual pizzas, with very inventive vegetarian toppings.

'They always have great soup here, and you can get a variety of fish,' Shay said to Deirdre, leaning close to her so that he could make himself heard above the general hum of conversation in the large open-plan restaurant. When she turned to look at him she met his curious glance, which held in it a veiled interest, as a man would look at a woman he found attractive. Deirdre felt his frision of interest and answering acute awareness in herself. She looked away instantly from his regard and pretended to study the menu, even though the print danced before her eyes and she could not take it in. His close proximity was all that she could think of…that and how vulnerable she had become to such interest, how much she needed that affirmation of her attractiveness, how much she needed empathetic male company.

Before she had made up her mind, the waiter was beside them and the children had placed their order in seconds. The waiter was looking at her expectantly.

'I…I'll have the soup of the day, please,' she said. 'And whatever fish you would recommend…the catch of the day, and a glass of white house wine.'

Perhaps, she thought as he made some squiggles on a note-pad, you could tell a lot about a person from the choices they made in restaurants. Her choice, she thought vaguely, would categorize her as a sensible, utilitarian woman, who was concerned about spending someone else's money. Certainly, you could tell a lot about the background of a person from their table manners. Such petty speculations distracted her for a moment or two from the deeper issues of her life. At the centre of her problems was the one of finding a man to love, someone who would want her with two children who were not her own. She did not think that her chances were very great of finding such a one. That realization filled her with despair. Sometimes she could visualize herself waiting until Mungo and Fleur were in university before she could find a husband for herself, could hope to have her own children. Perhaps then it would be too late.

Shay also ordered soup and fish, but not the specials of the day, and a glass of wine, though not the house wine. What that said about him was that he did not have to count the pennies, she thought, but he was not an extravagant man, given to excess. Deirdre was distracting herself from the inevitable confrontation with Jerry when they got back to the house and Shay would be gone.

When the waiter had gone, Shay turned to the children. 'Tell me about yourselves,' he invited. 'About your hobbies and interests.' Because he sounded genuinely interested—*was* interested—Deirdre warmed to him even more, while cautioning herself at the same time not to get used to having him around. Very soon he would be out of their lives and she would never see him again. This was one of those strange interludes in which fate gave you a glimpse of a world that might, remotely, be yours if circumstances could be different.

The children were taken aback and pleased that someone would ask them about their interests, because strangers usually asked them first what grade they were in at school, how they were doing at school, and so on. Then, usually, the eyes of those strangers would glaze with boredom when an attempt was made to give a genuine answer. The last thing they wanted to talk about was school. They wanted to get away from it, the academic worries that hung over them. Very quickly they were in an animated three-way conversation about horseriding, boating, hiking, drama, reading and so on, while Deirdre sat back and listened, quite happy to be in the background so that she could collect her muddled thoughts. This was the best part of a strange day.

When the food came, Shay turned his attention to her. 'May I call you Deirdre?' he asked. 'Or do you prefer Dee?'

'Deirdre,' she said. Only the children and a few old schoolfriends called her Dee. With this man she felt like a Deirdre…Deirdre of the Sorrows, as he had reminded her. That was her all right.

'Call me Shay,' he said. Again, he smiled at her as though she were an attractive woman. Sometimes these days she didn't think of herself as attractive, yet deep down she knew that she was. A lot of the time she felt herself to be more or less invisible where men were concerned. With her dark, glossy hair, that had hints of red in it, her pale, creamy skin and expressive hazel eyes she knew that she was not ordinary, yet most of the time now she could not feel otherwise. That was all part and parcel of low self-esteem, she knew, which had started from the time she had been laid off from the job that she had loved.

'When I was in front of Stanton Memorial this afternoon,' she heard herself saying, not having planned it, 'I saw that some positions for nurses were advertised. Specifically, operating room nurses. Do you…would you…perhaps know anything about that?'

'Well, I do know that the situation has changed in the time since you were laid off, mostly in the last six months. Most hospitals are looking for specialized nurses now. Many of the nurses who were laid off have gone to jobs in the United States, I suspect,' he said. 'They are just not there to be called back. Are you thinking of coming back?'

'Well, I…would like to. I haven't actually done anything about it,' she said carefully, not wanting to alarm Fleur and Mungo. 'I'm just thinking about how I could possibly do it.'

'Yes,' he said, understanding that she could not talk freely in front of the children. 'I could find out for you, if you would like me to. I know there's a shortage of nurses at Stanton. I operate there three days a week.'

'Thank you, I'd appreciate that,' she said. That would mean she would hear from him again, and even work with him if she got a job, if somehow she could combine being a mother to the children with a very demanding job in an operating suite. The idea of that lifted her spirits a few notches. It meant that she could go into the hospital and see a familiar face. Not that seeing him was the motivating factor—that would be an added bonus because he seemed like someone who would be good to work with. She had to get out from under.

'I'll see what I can do,' he said, just as Fleur and Mungo had taken their attention from the food they were eating and were looking at her and Shay with a quiet, speculative air. After being with them for two and a half years, Deirdre was attuned to the signals of their anxiety.

'It's all right,' she said, smiling at them, 'I'm not about to take off. Just thinking, perhaps, of getting a part-time job back in nursing, if there are any going.'

'That's a relief,' Fleur said. 'I think you should go for it, Dee. As long as you can still be with us.'

'I won't do anything without discussing it with you,' she said.

'Have you got kids?' Mungo chipped in, directing his attention to the man who sat opposite him. For some reason, Deirdre felt herself holding her breath. Mungo had an uncanny habit of asking pertinent questions at opportune moments.

'I have a fourteen-year-old son,' Shay said quietly. 'His name's Mark.' As he said that, there was a seriousness about him, Deirdre thought, a hesitancy. Quite suddenly there were vibes that she could not interpret. Perhaps he didn't like talking about his private life with strangers, even to the extent of telling them how many children he had—not like her, who had blurted out her problems. Well, he had invited her to do so, she defended herself. She was not secretive or stand-offish when it came to being honest about herself, although she was selective and careful about who heard her confidences.

So he was married. That was really a foregone conclusion, she thought. Such a pleasant, attractive man would be spoken for. He must be in his mid-thirties, she estimated, an established surgeon, it seemed.

For some reason she felt sad, a strange feeling like mourning, which she knew was part of her overall mental state of the moment. She felt herself slip back into that lonely world she had been in when she had sat on the bus and her body had refused to move.

'I could show you around the hospital, if you would like me to, Deirdre,' he said to her. 'And I could get permission from the head nurse of the operating suite and show you around there, too. She's a good person.'

'That would be very nice,' she managed to say. 'Thank you.'

'Give me your phone number before we leave here and I'll call you within the next few days,' he said.

'Thank you,' she said again, knowing that he was feeling sorry for her. So often men said they would call, and never did. Her sadness did not lift. If only her parents were there. They would not be back from Australia for at least another three months. Abruptly, she longed to see them.

Meanwhile, the invitation of this man seemed like a lifeline that she could cling to temporarily.

CHAPTER TWO

'WHERE the hell have you been?'

Jerry confronted them in the front hall of the house as they came in, having retrieved the four bags of groceries from the garage and then been dropped off at the front gate by Shay. They were in good spirits, having enjoyed the meal, until they saw Jerry, every inch the evil stepfather, Deirdre thought as she looked at him. Some of her sadness had gone, cheered by a single glass of house wine and the company of a good man. Now, looking at Jerry's red, thunderous face, some of it came back.

He was of medium height, broad and swarthy, with dark hair and eyes, with a certain primal attractiveness that some women found very attractive. Deirdre did not, although it had been his obvious expectation when they first met that she would find him so.

'We were invited out to eat,' she said, forcing calmness. 'Mungo left you a note, I think.' She was trying hard not to sound defensive or show her apprehension. Over the two and a half years that she had been with the family, she had vacillated between a rather low-key apprehension where he was concerned and a more or less indifferent tolerance. Always she was wary. That in itself had added to the strain. Now she was coming round to the idea that she wanted nothing more to do with him, something that was difficult when she was the substitute mother to his former wife's children.

'I got the note,' he said sharply, sarcastically. 'That may have been convenient for you, but I had colleagues in for drinks and they wanted something to eat.'

'I've decided,' Deirdre said, standing up straight to the extent of her five-foot-four frame, 'that I'm not going to cook for you any more, or your guests. It's too much for me. I was hired to look after the children, to cook for them, and that's what I'm going to do.'

'Bloody hell,' he said, his face suffusing even more with colour, 'you're getting above yourself. I could just fire you for that.'

Afterwards, Deirdre did not know how she mustered the courage to stand up to him. Her courage was of the quiet kind, which was slow to come but steely when roused.

'You do that, if it pleases you,' she said. 'I was hired by Mrs McGregor, so I don't think you are actually in a position to fire me. I've also decided to seek work as a nurse in a hospital, which is what I'm trained for. I'll still be a mother to the children, as I am now, but not with all the other work thrown in. It's time for me to go back to my real profession.'

It was as though she were still split into two people and the protective half was speaking for her, sounding firm, as though her mind had really been made up. It was amazing how her spirits lifted then, bringing such a rush of relief that she could almost have laughed aloud at the comic expression of fury on Jerry's face.

'Come on, kids,' she said to Mungo and Fleur. 'Please, help me to put the groceries away.' The three of them marched into the kitchen, with the children's stepfather coming after them. Quickly, they began to put things away.

Jerry moved close to Deirdre and with two fingers extended used them to push her shoulder, push her back against a wall.

'You little bitch,' he said. 'You've got a good job here and a home, and you can't do a bit of cooking for me.'

'I have a home of my own,' she said, referring to her parents' modest bungalow, which was also her permanent home, that she was taking care of while they were out of the country. Not for the first time she was overwhelmingly grateful that she had it. 'I also have a profession that I can return to. I've no intention of giving up the children. I'm sure that Mrs McGregor and I can come to some arrangement that is to our mutual benefit.' It was as though her mind had made itself up, without any obvious conscious input. What a relief that all this was coming out, even though her heart was beating fast in the knowledge that she might have to take flight. 'And don't touch me, don't threaten me.'

Mungo and Fleur moved closer to her, as though both to seek protection and to offer it.

'Don't talk to me like that,' he shouted at her, 'as though I don't figure in the equation. I have a say about who comes into this house. I can get another nanny, maybe someone who would be only too happy to marry me, have this house as a home, be more grateful than you are.'

'That was never part of the arrangement where I was concerned,' Deirdre said calmly, through the familiar sick fear. It was possible that if he married, he could fight the grandmother for custody of the children. After all, she was elderly, did not have the energy to take on the children herself, to move them into her own home, which was why she had hired a nanny in the first place. Deirdre did not doubt that Fiona McGregor would do so if the threat became real. First thing in the morning she would call her and ask to talk with her about her desire to return to nursing.

Again, Jerry stabbed at her with his fingers, to emphasize each word. 'Don't think that you're indispensable, Miss High-and-Mighty. People like you are two a penny.'

'I think not,' she said, with admirable dignity. 'In fact, it's the other way round. People like me are rare. It's not trendy to do what I'm doing, not cool, far from the limelight.'

'No, they're not!' Fleur chipped in, her thin face pale. 'She's special. We want Dee with us.'

'And don't you threaten her,' Mungo said, gaining courage from his sister. 'I'll talk to the social worker at school and tell her that you've been verbally abusive, that you pushed Dee. That won't go down very well with the authorities. We're old enough to have a say about who we live with, who our legal guardians are.'

'You two get upstairs and get on with your homework!' Jerry shouted at them, pointing out to the staircase in the hall.

'We're not going anywhere until we know that Dee's all right,' Mungo said, his voice quavering a little, and Deirdre felt a rush of love for both the children. Although she was close to tears, there was no way that she would give this man the satisfaction of seeing it.

'That's right. You leave her alone,' Fleur said. She linked her hand through Deirdre's. 'Come upstairs with us, Dee. I need some help with something.'

The three of them went out of the kitchen and began to go up the staircase.

'As far as I'm concerned, you're fired,' Jerry shouted after them.

'No, she's not,' Mungo said. 'We want her with us.'

In Fleur's bedroom, with the door locked, they all sat on the bed. 'What are we going to do?' Fleur whispered, sounding close to tears. 'I couldn't bear it if you weren't with us, Dee.'

'I shall be with you,' Deirdre said as firmly as she could

manage. 'I'm going to call your granny and talk to her about it, see if I can meet her tomorrow. You can discuss things better with people face to face. I'll do it tonight, not wait until tomorrow. I'll see her in the morning. It's time to get very serious. If Jerry gets too much, you can live with her, or with me in my house. Granny has plenty of space. Also, I'm going to talk to a lawyer about the fact that Jerry pushed me—I know someone—so that it's on record, in case I need that.' At that moment she was not sure exactly how she would need it, but an instinct told her that it was a good thing to have a record of what had happened between them. Her situation was odd. She really had no claim on the children, she was simply an employee, yet she knew that Jerry Parks was not good for them.

'We're going to talk to the social worker at school tomorrow,' Fleur said, 'so that's on record there, too.'

'Yes. Why did you suddenly think about going back to work as a nurse, Dee?' Mungo asked. 'I mean, why today? Has something happened?'

'Not specifically,' Deirdre said slowly, searching for words. 'It's something I've been thinking about for some time, because what has happened here is that I've taken on more and more of the job of housekeeper and hostess, when I don't want to be that, instead of just taking care of you. I've stuck it out because I thought he might ask me to go…and I think you need me.'

There, it was out. The breakdown that she feared still threatened her, yet somehow it seemed less acute because she had articulated her thoughts and needs, had had a showdown of sorts. Inside, she felt as though she were trembling. What she could not say to them at this time was that one day she hoped to have a husband and children of her own, and who would take her on if she were the mother of two children who were not her own? If she were to wait until Mungo and Fleur were old enough to go to university, and off her hands, she would be in her early thirties, which seemed impossibly in the future. At the moment she could only project herself forward for the next six months or so.

Fleur began to weep. 'We do need you,' she managed to get out, between sobs. 'I couldn't bear it if you went.'

'Don't go, Dee,' Mungo said.

Deirdre's own eyes pricked with tears and she swallowed, her throat tight with emotion. 'I'm not going,' she said. 'We're going to work it all out. Sometimes you come to a point in your life when you have to make changes, and there's no sense in putting it off because it will just go on nagging and nagging you. I would prefer not to have anything whatsoever to do with Jerry Parks, don't want to see him even.'

They sat together, their arms around each other. They could hear Jerry down below, crashing about as though he were throwing cooking pots. Maybe he was, Deirdre speculated, and found that she didn't care.

'Look,' she said at length, 'you two get on with your homework. I'm going to phone Granny. I'll come in a little while to help you, Fleur. Try not to worry. We are going to work something out, and I'm not going to accept a job in nursing until everything with us is working well…if I ever get offered anything, that is.'

'Will you sleep here tonight, Dee?' Fleur asked.

'Yes,' she said. Quite often she slept at her parents' home, a modest place that was a relatively short distance away on the edge of a less affluent area.

In the bedroom that was hers in this house, she locked the door, a habit that she had acquired ever since the unwanted encounter with a semi-drunk Jerry when she had first come to the house, when he had entered her room one night and tried to force himself on her. Then and there she had almost left, almost thrown her few belongings into her suitcase and rushed out. Only the images of the two young, unhappy faces had prevented her.

Using her mobile phone, she called Fiona McGregor, having decided not to wait until the morning. A sense of urgency made her edgy. 'Hello, Mrs McGregor. This is Deirdre.'

'Oh, hello, Deirdre, my dear. How are you? Now, you are supposed to call me Fiona.' The good-natured voice came back. Granny McGregor could be tart when annoyed, but never mean or unfair.

'I know,' Deirdre said, smiling, not wanting to tell her employer that she always thought of her as 'Granny McGregor'. 'I'm calling to ask if I could possibly come to see you tomorrow, Fiona. I've been thinking of going back to nursing, and I want to work out with you how I might do that and continue to look after the children.'

'Well, my dear, I'm not really surprised. I've seen this coming on for some time, but I didn't want to say anything until you had worked it out in your own mind. It seems you have done so now. I just hope that you won't leave us, because the children love you so and would be lost without you. So would I.'

For the second time that evening, the relief of having unburdened herself to someone who could understand was overwhelming. It began to seem very odd to Deirdre now that she had not sought out this help before. Somehow she had got it into her head that she had to do it all herself. Fiona, she knew, was still mourning for her daughter. Meeting Shay had had something to do with this surge of courage as well.

'Perhaps I shouldn't have waited to say something,' Fiona was going on. 'I think you're upset. Am I right?'

'Yes,' Deirdre said, her voice low.

'I suspect that you've had just about as much of Jerry Parks as you can stand. Right?'

'Right.'

'Well, we'll do something about it. Come tomorrow, at any time that's convenient to you, dear,' Fiona said. 'There are one or two things I want to clear up with you as well, things that perhaps I should have told you before, but which I wanted to leave until we had all tested you out, myself and the children, then they got put off indefinitely. You've been a wonderful mother to the children, you've brought some sanity and stability to their lives. If my daughter were alive, she'd be the first to say that, so I want to thank you, Deirdre.'

Deirdre wanted to cry. By a supreme effort she found her voice. 'I'll come at eleven o'clock, if that's all right?' she said.

'That's perfect. I'll give you something to think about before you come. You'll remember that I told you my daughter had won some money in a lottery, just before she got sick? The irony of it! Well, it's much more than I gave you to believe. She got sixteen million dollars. That's why friend Jerry is hanging around. He would have been up and out long ago, believe me. The last thing he wanted was to look after children that were not even his own, although I suspect that he would be the same with his own children.'

'That makes it clearer,' Deirdre said. 'I understand more now.' It had long been a mystery to her why Jerry, impatient and ill at ease with the children, should make a pretence of being there for them.

'There's a court case on to prevent him getting his hands on the money, because Moira had filed for divorce from Jerry before she knew she had won the money, and he had signed the papers agreeing to the divorce,' Fiona went on, somewhat wearily. 'That's crucial, you see. Otherwise she would automatically have had to share the money equally with her husband. She couldn't stand to be with him any longer. He used to hit her, you know. I think he envied her because she was a successful artist, that she could do something good with her own talent.'

'I…I didn't know, of course,' Deirdre said. 'But I'm not surprised.'

'That's the only reason he's hanging about,' Fiona McGregor repeated bitterly, 'pretending to be a father to the children.'

'So the divorce was finalized?' Deirdre asked hesitantly, not knowing the ins and out of divorce.

'Yes…just. But she won the money before it was finalized, so Jerry is saying that he should have half of it. Then Moira became too ill, and deteriorated very quickly, before actually getting around to selling the house and other assets or trying to fight him.'

'I see,' Deirdre said, although it all sounded very convoluted and complicated, and she was not sure that she wanted to know all that.

'She didn't have the energy to do anything else, but her intentions were certainly known to her lawyer,' Fiona went on sadly. 'She had a will, leaving most of her estate to the children and something to me. Jerry has been trying to get it ever since, and doesn't want to let go of the children for that reason.' She gave a derisive laugh. 'Otherwise, with no money, he would have been out of there before you could say "knife". Certainly he would have left before she died…he didn't want to have anything to do with her illness. All these legal things pending are the only reasons that he hasn't brought a woman into the home, someone to live with him, not just as a nanny to the children. He wants to present a good image.'

'I see.'

'Thank God I'm their legal guardian under Moira's will. Jerry owns half that house, so he's pretty well off in his own right. I'll fill you in on more of the details tomorrow,' Fiona promised.

'Do the children know how much money there is?' Deirdre asked.

'No, I thought it better not to tell them the amount yet. It might make them think that they don't have to make an effort in life. Though they're pretty good kids, work hard at school.'

'Yes…' she said.

'Where were you thinking of applying for a nursing job?'

'Well, I just walked by the Stanton Memorial Hospital today and saw a notice that they need operating room nurses. I thought maybe I would try there,' Deirdre said. 'It was just a spur-of-the-moment thing, but I've been thinking for some time that I ought to take some action.'

'You're right, dear. We'll talk tomorrow about that as well, shall we? We should have done this a while ago.'

'Yes.'

'You have to be quite sure that you can cope with it, dear…taking on a job in nursing and wanting to stay with the children, too. Of course, I'll do more. I should have done more from the beginning. Are you sure it won't be too much for you?'

'I'm not sure, but I want both. The nursing job would be part of my individual life. Don't you see?'

'Yes, dear, I think I do. I blame myself for not seeing it coming. Perhaps I've taken you too much for granted, although I've tried not to.'

'Don't blame yourself,' Deirdre said: 'We'll talk tomorrow.'

'Goodnight, then, dear. Keep your mobile phone with you at all times. You call me right away if there's any trouble with you-know-who, and I'll come round there, with the police in tow if necessary. It's a good idea to get an official report if you get threatened.'

'Thank you. Goodnight.' It had been good for her to talk to Fiona, who had suffered the loss of her only daughter whom she had loved desperately, so she had said. That event must be something that was always on her mind. Between them they would sort out something that was good for her daughter's children.

Thoughtfully Deirdre sat on her bed and stared at the locked door. Things were falling into place. It had long puzzled her why a self-centred, impatient man like Jerry would go through the motions of being a father when his heart and his talents were very obviously not in that direction. As for herself, she had only been able to tolerate the situation because he was away a lot, travelling overseas in connection with his work, mostly to Third World countries, involved in sweat-shop manufacturing, she thought. The house was just sort of a hotel to him, where he expected service and comfort, rather than a home to which he should contribute something.

She wondered how Moira could ever have got involved with someone like Jerry. Perhaps he had offered her material things at a time when her own profession had been precarious and she had had the two children to support. Those children were the products of Moira's idealistic student days, it seemed, when love and attraction had taken precedence over birth control and common sense.

What irony that Moira had won millions in a lottery just before she had contracted a terminal illness.

Deirdre's mobile phone, on the bed beside her, shrilled.

'Hi! This is Shay Melburne,' the now familiar voice said. 'I decided to give you a call because I've been wondering if you are all right, in view of the fact that you didn't want to enter the house earlier in the evening.'

'Oh, hello,' Deirdre said, blushing and absurdly pleased to hear his voice, even though she knew that he was forbidden to her, so to speak, being married. 'That's kind of you.

I…well…there has been a showdown of sorts, but it's going to be all right, I think. I'm going to see the children's grandmother tomorrow, who's my real employer.'

'And that will be all right, you think?' his pleasant, calm voice enquired.

'I think it will clarify the situation for me,' she said.

'My second reason for calling,' he said, his tone light, 'is from a morbid curiosity to find out if Basil the rat got into your groceries in the garage.'

As he had, no doubt, intended, she laughed. 'No, everything was intact,' she said. 'Sweet of you to ask, though.'

'I'm also calling to see if you would like to come to the hospital tomorrow, maybe at lunchtime. I could meet you in the main lobby, we could have lunch in the hospital cafeteria, maybe, and then I could show you the operating suite…with the permission of the head nurse. I'm not actually operating tomorrow, but I do have to see some patients in the outpatients department in the morning.'

The glow of pleasure that suffused her made it plain that there was no way she would refuse such a wonderful opportunity. Things were moving quickly. Perhaps getting to breaking point and then taking action always moved things along in this way when you found yourself at an impasse. 'Well…I have to see my employer at eleven o'clock tomorrow,' she said hesitantly, 'and expect to be with her for at least an hour…'

'Would one o'clock be all right?'

'Yes. Thank you, I really appreciate that.'

'My pleasure. See you tomorrow, then. Are you sure that everything's all right?' Even though he scarcely knew her, he was obviously picking up vibes or something, she thought, from the tone of her voice.

'There's nothing I can't cope with,' she said, lying, forcing a lightness to her voice. 'Goodnight.'

'Goodnight.' It seemed to her that he sounded reluctant to hang up.

Perhaps the act of nearly running her over was on his conscience, so that he felt an exaggerated responsibility for her, she speculated. It was good that he did. She sat there on the bed glowing with an unaccustomed sense of being cared for. Having had to stand on her own two feet for so long had made her feel like a wary, hunted animal a lot of the time when things went wrong. Partly, she suspected, because she didn't always know how to ask for help, where to go, whom she could trust.

In her experience, so many people backed off from real need. It frightened them, even some individuals whose job it was to help in the 'caring professions'. It was so much easier to give at a distance, to give money to famine relief in distant lands, for instance, than to help a friend, neighbour or acquaintance who was suffering from depression and slowly going under. That was something she had observed frequently in her young life, all the more amazing to her because she jumped into the fray herself, got her hands dirty, so to speak.

The euphoric glow was short-lived as she heard the heavy tread of Jerry on the stairs. His bedroom, thank God, was not on the second floor. He had his own suite at ground level. Life would not have been bearable otherwise, for herself or for the children. He thumped on the door with a fist. Then the knob turned. Thank God she had got into the habit of always keeping it locked.

'I want to talk to you,' he said.

'I'll see you in the morning, early. Half past seven,' she said.

He was swearing, loud enough for her to hear. Then she heard him going down the stairs. Perhaps tomorrow he would try to fire her again. Well, it was not the end of the world. She would move back home, she had very few clothes or other things here, and the children would go to their grandmother, while she, Deirdre, would continue to be a mother to them. Then Jerry would go away again on one of his trips that could last for several weeks.

Breathing deeply to calm herself and slow her rapidly beating heart, she planned her next moves. Now she would help the children with their homework, if needed, supervise their bedtime, then have a bath herself, put out her clothes for the next day and then go to bed.

Deirdre had known that she would not sleep well. Too much had happened that day for her to attain peace of mind, yet it was a sleeplessness of a different sort now, because it had the excitement of possibility in it, a hope of better things.

Lying there, she was haunted by the image of Jerry coming into the room when she had been new to the job, when she had been in the house for only two weeks. He had come in late at night and flung himself onto the bed, partially on top of her, smelling of alcohol, grinning at her in the expectation that she would welcome him.

The look of horror on her face had got through to him, inebriated as he had been, and she had easily drawn up her knees and kicked him off her. She had run from the room, managing to snatch up her handbag with her cellphone in it, then her coat and outdoor shoes from by the front door as she had run out of the house. Out in the front garden where she could yell for help to the neighbours, she had told Jerry, who had come after her eventually, that she would not come back into the house until he had gone to his own quarters. She had had her phone in her hand, had threatened to call the police. Now she knew that he had not persisted because he could not risk being known to the police when he wanted to get his hands on the money that Moira had left.

How mixed up and sordid it all seemed. Yet in spite of all that, what shone through was the innate sweetness of the children, their desperate need and appreciation of her. As though they were her own flesh and blood, that was what anchored her in this place.

Deirdre closed her eyes, willing herself to think of other things. The image of another man came to mind, a man with grey, curious eyes, who looked at her as though he saw her as she was, fully human, as well as an attractive woman. He had looked at her in the way she saw herself when she felt herself to be at her best—not Deirdre of the Sorrows, but Deirdre of the joy. That had been reflected in him. Even though he was married and had a son, could not be anything to her other than, at best, a casual friend and perhaps professional colleague, his advent in her life had left her with something very positive. It made her smile.

CHAPTER THREE

THE hospital front lobby of the main building of Stanton Memorial was smaller and on a more human scale than the main lobby at University Hospital in downtown Prospect Bay, Deirdre thought as she entered and looked around her.

Taking off her hat, scarf and gloves and unbuttoning her warm raincoat, she looked quickly for Shay, as she ran a hand through her hair. It was a raw, wet day, one of those days when it was difficult to look smartly dressed, and she had come by bus. There was no sign of him. It was shortly before one o'clock.

There was a gift shop off to one side, with the usual teddy bears, other toys and useful items that individuals might need when they were patients in a hospital, as well as the usual buckets of fresh flowers on the floor outside. It was nice to be in a hospital again, provided that you were there to work, were not sick yourself or visiting someone who was sick. When you or your family needed the services of a hospital, it was a different story. You saw things and were sensitive to nuances of attitude that you seldom, if ever, noticed when you simply worked there. Deirdre knew that well, since her father has been sick.

'Can I be of any help to you?' a voice enquired, and Deirdre looked at the elderly woman in a pale blue overall who had asked the question. Pinned to the front of her uniform she had a large, round badge with the words PLEASE ASK ME. I'M A VOLUNTEER. RUTH.

Deirdre smiled in answer to the other woman's smile, well appreciating the value of volunteers in a setting that could be impersonal and bewildering. 'I'm supposed to meet someone here in the lobby,' she said. 'A Dr Melburne. Is there some-where I could sit? He should be here very soon.'

'There's a bench over there, at the side of the gift shop,' the woman pointed. 'And if you'd like a coffee, there's a lit-tle refreshment booth over there.'

Deirdre seated herself on the bench and looked around her keenly. Already the ambience of the place had given her a fa-vourable impression. It was amazing how much you could tell about a place in a short while, whether it was going to be cold and impersonal, or more patient-centred and warm on a human scale. The very fact that they used volunteers up front told her something positive.

She saw Shay before he saw her, as he came into the lobby from a side corridor. He was wearing the uniform of the op-erating room, a two-piece green scrub suit, with a white lab coat over the top, which made him look even more attractive than he had seemed to her yesterday in street clothes, yet at the same time more remote. His short, simply cut hair looked smooth and glossy with health.

Looking at him now, unaware of her as he was, she won-dered how she could have abandoned herself to pouring out most of her troubles to him, a complete stranger. Surely he would not be the slightest bit interested in her troubles, even though he had listened to her attentively. At the thought, her cheeks warmed with a certain embarrassment. Yet he had asked her...had seemed very sincere in his desire to help. And he had called her last night. The subsequent relief had been so wonderful. Embarrassed or not, there was no point in regretting that, she told herself, her internal dialogue chattering away in full swing.

The jolt of recognition that she felt when she saw him sent her heart beating faster and she chastised herself for being so attracted to him, a man who was not free. If he had been free, she told herself, he would most likely not be interested in her anyway, a young woman who was the mother of someone else's children, who had painted herself into a corner, as he had put it, who had been out of nursing for two and a half years and was out of touch with the professional world that she had once inhabited.

It was more clear to her now that when she had taken the job to look after the children she had not had any idea that Jerry would prove to be such an inadequate, reluctant, more or less non-existent father. She had assumed at the time that she would not be taking on the role of single parent, which it had turned out to be. She had simply assumed that her job would be temporary and that she would go back to her profession and perhaps remain a friend of the family so that Mungo and Fleur had some continuity in their lives. Maybe Fiona should have told her that…if she had known the full extent of his neglect herself.

The moral of that story was not to assume…

As Deirdre stared at the man, she thought that there was not much she could offer a sophisticated, accomplished man like Shay Melburne—except her sincerity, honesty, all the positive attributes of character and personality that she thought she possessed. She was for the most part a quiet and modest person, she thought, one not given to blowing her own trumpet. Now, of course, she knew more or less all there was to know about running a home efficiently, and she had become a very good cook as well. She

wasn't a bad mother either. Those were not accomplish-
ments to be sneezed at, although she knew that society in
general did not put a high premium on those skills because
they were often taken for granted, behind the scenes as
they were, yet they were becoming rarer by the year, it
seemed to her. Not that she would be in a position to offer
him anything…

Smiling wryly to herself, she pushed those thoughts out of
her mind. As she half rose to go forward to greet him, another
man, a colleague attired in the same professional garb, came
from another direction and accosted him. 'Hi, Shay! How are
you? Good to see you.'

'Hi, Tom. I'm pretty good. Haven't seen you for a while.'

'I was in Prague for the conference. Lynne came with me
and we decided to make a vacation out of it. We stayed for a
month. I thought you might have been there.'

'Couldn't make it this time.'

'Pity. It was great. How is Mark?'

'He's improving, I'm relieved to say.'

'I'm glad to hear it. Well, I'll see you upstairs, no doubt.'

'No doubt, Tom.'

Deirdre had sat down again on the bench, not wanting to
appear to be privy to the conversation which had been private.
But because surgeons often tended to speak in loud, booming
voices—and Shay Melburne's colleague was no exception—
it had been accessible to anyone who had cared to take note
of it, although Shay's contribution had been more subdued. As
she looked around her, she could not see anyone else who
might have been interested. They were all hurrying about their
business. Mark, she knew, was the name of his fourteen-year-
old son. Was he ill? She did not know Shay well enough to ask,
and although she had unburdened herself to him, it was not
likely that he needed to do the same where she was concerned.

He saw her and smiled when she moved forward to greet him. 'Good afternoon, Dr Melburne,' she said.

He extended a hand to her and they shook hands formally, a gesture that for some reason brought a lump to her throat. She had got the distinct, subtle impression that he had wanted to touch her and that the handshake was the only way. For her part, she had felt the urge to sway forward against him so that he could hug her. The idea of it sobered her. In the space of a very short time she had come to feel a sense that she was relying on him. That would not do. Even if they were to work together, if luck were with her there, it would be a professional relationship.

'Good afternoon, Deirdre,' he said, looking at her searchingly. 'I hope that all is well with you?'

'Yes, it is.'

'Good. This is a nice time to go to the cafeteria, if you're hungry,' he said. 'The first lunch rush will be over. It's on this level.'

Deirdre nodded, feeling suddenly tongue-tied.

Within a very short time they were seated at a table in the spacious cafeteria, where Deirdre had chosen a sandwich and a glass of orange juice, with their trays before them.

'I've arranged with the head of the operating room for me to show you around,' he said. 'We have to be there in precisely twenty minutes, which doesn't give us much time to gobble this food.'

'I'd forgotten how rushed everything often is in a hospital,' she said, smiling tentatively at him across the expanse of the table. 'Constantly watching the clock and having deadlines throughout the day.'

'Yes, I expect you get out of it after a while, then you have to make an effort to get back in. Maybe we'll do a test. We'll start with giving you two minutes to change into a scrub suit in the nurses' change room. How about that?' The smile he gave her made her heart do a little flip.

'I think I could make it,' she said. An almost forgotten feeling of happiness, euphoria, came over her.

It seemed amazing that less than twenty-four hours ago she had not known he existed, had sat like a zombie on a bus, unable to move. It was also amazing how quickly your life could be changed, for better or worse, if you took certain steps. Probably she would have contacted the human resources department on her own about jobs if she had not met Shay Melburne, but it would have taken longer and certainly would not have been so pleasurable. Not that she deluded herself that she was over her depression yet, or whatever it was, in spite of the positive effect of her companion. Something like that took time to work through. She would give herself that time, yet take action as well, she resolved there and then.

'Good. I'll show you where the change room is, then there are piles of uniforms inside and the disposable overshoes that you can just put on over your regular shoes. Remember?' He grinned at her.

'Yes, I do.' She grinned back. 'I'm looking forward to it. I...I'm really grateful to you for setting this up, Dr Melburne.'

'I just hope it works out for you, if you decide it's what you want,' he said. 'Please, call me Shay.'

They ate quickly and talked at the same time. 'You mentioned to me last night that you were going to see the children's grandmother,' he said.

'Yes. I did go this morning. We've sorted out some things. If the children really don't want to go on living in the same house as Jerry, they can move in with her. But, of course, the house they are in now is bigger and nicer, and he's away a lot, but they are going to have the option, and will move over some of their clothes and other things, to be ready if he gets worse. So far he hasn't been physically abusive to them, thank goodness. They stay at my parents' house with me, too, fairly frequently.'

There was the other concern that she was not sure she should, or could, tell him, something that she could not make up her mind about because it would have a profound effect on her life. How could she tell him, this virtual stranger, that she was apprehensive that she would not be able to have a husband and children of her own.

'And?' he said, stopping in the act of finishing off his food, looking at her very astutely, so that she found herself blushing. It was uncanny that he seemed to read her mind on such a short acquaintance.

'How do you know that there is an "and"?' she said.

'In the short time that we've known each other,' he said, 'I've come to interpret the nuances of your reactions, Deirdre,' he said, smiling slightly.

'That's a little scary,' she said.

'A matter of acute observation,' he said, smiling again so that such a reply would not seem pompous.

'Um…there was one other thing,' she said in a rush, deciding to tell him. 'She—Mrs McGregor—asked me if I would agree to be legal guardian to the children if she were to become incapacitated…or die in the near future.' She looked down at her plate, remembering the shock of being asked, not knowing what to say. 'She's a lovely person, I really like her. I really don't want to think of her as not being around.'

'And what did you tell her?' he probed gently.

'Well, I couldn't make up my mind then and there,' she said, looking up at him. 'I…I told her I would think it over. There's no hurry, because she's in good health, but she obviously wants to get it settled. But I…I don't think Jerry would allow that. He would fight. It's very complex. It's not as though he cares for the children—he doesn't. I don't know what to do.'

'Hmm,' he murmured thoughtfully. 'If you'd like to talk about it some more later, Deirdre, I would be very happy to listen and maybe offer my two cents' worth. Right now we have to rush up to the operating suite.'

Deirdre welcomed the sudden change of pace as they walked quickly to the elevators and went up to the second floor of the wing where the operating suite was situated. It made her feel exhilarated to be in a crowded elevator with hospital personnel again—talking to each other, greeting colleagues, laughing—and made her once again realize how isolated she had become. Here she was, back in an adult world that she understood, where her skills would, perhaps, once again be valued…if she was lucky.

'Two minutes. Remember?' Shay instructed her as they came to a room outside the main part of the operating suite, which he told her was the nurses' change room. He looked at his watch to indicate that he was timing her.

When she found herself laughing, Deirdre was struck again at how strange it was that yesterday she had been in despair and then in such a short time her world was beginning to change.

There was no one else in the change room and she quickly looked around for a locker with a key and flung her things into it, then picked up a light blue scrub suit, a paper hat to put over her hair and soft paper overshoes. This was just like old times, she thought as she stripped off her sweater and skirt and quickly got into the scrub suit. Not bothering to look at her watch, she knew that she was within the two minutes when she opened the door to join Shay.

'Great!' he said, as she came out, his eyes lighting up, his eyebrows raised at the sight of her. For a brief moment her eyes locked with his and she found herself colouring at his obvious appraisal, smiling back as he smiled at her. Then she looked away quickly as a frision of awareness overlaid the camaraderie that they had shared, which had nonetheless remained somewhat formal, for all its apparent casualness.

Instantly she knew that in her vulnerable state she was in danger of falling in love with him, or at least getting a schoolgirl crush on him, which was not appropriate as she was now a woman.

'Come on,' he said, giving no sign that he had noticed her colour. 'I'll introduce you to the head nurse. Her name's Darlene Reade and she's been here a long time.'

The head nurse's small office, like a command post, which was the purpose it served, was just inside the main double doors of the operating suite, over to one side. Directly in front of them, as they entered, was a desk for the main receptionist, who vetted everyone who entered the suite.

'Hello, Bev,' Shay addressed the receptionist, a blonde woman of about forty, while he deftly took a paper cap from a pile and put it on his head, then took a disposable paper mask for himself and handed one to Deirdre. 'This is Deirdre Warwick, RN, who's come to have a quick tour of the OR. Deirdre, this is Bev, who knows everyone and knows everything that's going on here, at all times.'

'Pleased to meet you, Deirdre,' Bev said, standing up to shake her hand. 'Are you coming to work here?'

'That depends,' Deirdre said, 'on what I find here…and whether anyone would want me.' When she smiled at the receptionist she was very aware of how her confidence had risen a few notches as Shay had referred to her qualification—it had been a long time since anyone had introduced her as an RN.

'You'll be wanted. Darlene's in her office, so you'd better grab her before she disappears. This has been a hectic day so far.'

They went through the same process with the head nurse in her office. Darlene Reade could have been anywhere from forty-five to over sixty, Deirdre thought, viewing the tired, pale face of the head nurse who nonetheless looked cheerful and welcoming, if harried.

'You go ahead, Shay,' she said, after shaking hands with Deirdre. 'I'm pretty well tied up here. We've had more than our fair share of emergencies.' When one of the office telephones shrilled, Shay took Deirdre's arm and they left.

'Put your mask on,' he said, 'then we can be anonymous. At least, you can. I'll show you around generally, we won't go into any rooms where there's an operation in progress.'

When she tied on the rather stiff paper mask, her hands felt clumsy with a certain nervousness, not least because she found that she wanted very much to impress Shay, but feared that she was out of touch and would need a refresher course.

He showed her everything—the stockrooms, the clean instrument room where trays of instruments were packed and sterilized for specific operations, the dirty instrument room where used instruments were washed and sterilized by specially trained staff. The central supply unit was thus part of the operating suite, yet separate from it. Then they went on to the operating rooms themselves, each with a scrub area outside, of sinks where the surgeons and the nurses scrubbed before an operation.

'I do mainly general surgery,' he informed her. 'And this room, number one, is where I usually operate on Mondays, Wednesdays and Fridays.'

'I see,' she said, looking through a small communication window off the scrub area so that she could see inside the room where an operation was in progress. 'It's so nice to be back in an operating room. Is that a gut resection they're doing?'

Shay moved up close behind her to look over her shoulder, so that suddenly she was acutely aware of his physical presence just inches away from her. Swallowing nervously, she stared straight ahead. 'It looks like it,' he said. 'There's an operating list over here.'

Beside the entrance door to each operating room, the operating list for the day was posted on the wall. Shay ran his finger down it. 'Yes...look,' he said, putting a hand on her shoulder and drawing her over beside him to view the long list of operations that were on the agenda for that day, many of which had already been done. 'It is a gut resection.'

Aware of nothing other than his touch, Deirdre stared blindly at the list. Then he dropped his hand, having touched her for no longer than a few seconds, not long enough for it to be suggestive or offensive had she not liked him. He was simply being attentive and kind, Deirdre knew, and it was having a devastating effect on her, starved for affection and attention as she was. Hoping that wasn't too obvious, she searched her mind for something to say.

'Well...you certainly get through a lot of work here,' she managed to get out.

All too soon the tour was over and they were back at the main entrance. 'Thank you so much,' she said. 'I like the atmosphere of the place.' All along, other members of the staff had spoken warmly to Shay and had greeted her warmly also when introduced. Her first impressions were that this department was very professional, very efficient, very busy and a good place in which to work. 'There seems to be a good team spirit.'

'There is,' he agreed. 'Would you like a cup of coffee? We could get one in the main lobby. There's a coffee-lounge up here in the OR, but the coffee at this time of the day leaves something to be desired. I'm parched myself.'

'I'd like that,' she said, her heart lifting at the prospect of spending a little more time with him, as the thought that she might not see him again for a long time had tempered her previous light mood as the tour had wound up.

They walked back to the nurses' change room. 'Two minutes?' she said to him.

'I'll give you three this time,' he said, grinning.

The time that it took her to comb her hair and put on a little make-up after she had changed back into street clothes took up the three minutes.

She felt awkward with him as they went down in the elevator to the lobby again, worrying about how to thank him finally and how to say goodbye. The thought of having to say goodbye depressed her.

'If you think you would like to work here, Deirdre, I can direct you to the human resources department to pick up an application form,' he said when they were in the lobby, walking towards the tiny coffee-shop. 'It's down that way. Follow the signs. What sort of coffee will you have? This is my treat.'

'I'll have a *latté* with soy milk, small, please…if they have it,' she said.

'They have it.'

Carrying the two cups of coffee, he headed for the main doors. 'Do you mind if we get a bit of fresh air? It's not too cold, I hope.'

'I don't mind.' She was warmly dressed, while he had only a cotton lab coat over his scrub suit. The entrance was sheltered from the light drizzle, and they moved to one side of the main doors.

It was good to stand there with him in the cool, brisk air, with her hand round the warm paper cup. They were more or less alone for now.

'Well…' he began, 'do you think you will apply to work here, Deirdre? It's a good place.'

'I think I will apply,' she said pensively. 'I have a few things to work out first—in my head, as well as from a practical point of view.'

'Yes, I think you do,' he agreed.

'I…I couldn't work here until other things were working smoothly. I don't want to bore you with all my difficulties. You've been very kind and patient.' She sipped her coffee pensively, staring out into the rain-slicked street, having the sense that they were enclosed in a little world of their own, from which she did not wish to extricate herself.

'You don't bore me, Deirdre,' he said softly. 'I've enjoyed showing you around. Will you have dinner with me again some time soon?'

'I…well…' she said, her heart beating more quickly. More than anything she wanted to have dinner with him. In fact, she clung to the possibility that she would be able to see him again. But she couldn't do it. 'I don't think it would be a good idea for me to go out to dinner with a married man. You see, I'm too susceptible to…um…your attention, and I might make a fool of myself.'

Surprising her, he flung back his head and laughed. 'I wish you would make a fool of yourself with me, Deirdre of the Sorrows,' he said. 'As for being married, I'm not. I was married once, now I'm divorced. I'm not proud of that. My wife left me. She's now living with a sheep farmer in New Zealand. She met him over here while she was working as a physiotherapist and he was on holiday from the sheep. He had an accident in his car, touring the back country, and as a consequence of that he eventually met my wife in the course of his treatment. I guess she went for his rugged masculinity, not to mention the time and attention that he paid her.'

This time it was her turn to laugh, such was her relief and the comic nature of his description. 'I shouldn't laugh,' she apologized. 'Do you mind—about the divorce, I mean?'

'I minded at the time, particularly for my son. Now I don't. I have custody of Mark. Sometimes he misses his mother,' he said, a new note of regret coming into his voice.

'It's sad,' she said.

'It was my fault,' he said. 'I suppose one could describe me as having been a workaholic…not an easy thing for a wife to have to deal with. She, Tony—short for Antonia—used to call me "the twenty-four-seven man" where work was concerned. She was quite right there.'

'And now?' Deirdre enquired softly, turning to look at him.

'I'm learning to temper my ambitious drive, you might say,' he replied, an odd note of bitterness in his voice.

She wanted to ask him about his son, about the remark that his colleague had made, but knew it was too soon and that it was not her business to ask. If he wanted her to know, he would tell her. For a few moments they sipped their coffee in silence.

'It's not enough to be in love,' he said very quietly, as though talking to himself. 'You've got to have staying power…and a lot more besides. Anyone can go through a wedding ceremony. It's what comes after that's the test, the day-to-day living, the daily grind.'

'Yes.'

'One needs tolerance and forgiveness,' he said. 'That is, the ability to display those qualities, to feel them. I think it was the poet Goethe who said something about love being an ideal thing, marriage a real thing. One must be easy to live with, and all that that implies—consideration, kindness, respecting the other's privacy, sharing the tedious chores of life, good manners, thoughtfulness, integrity… The list goes on. In short, I suppose it adds up to maturity, which is not particularly common.'

'Yes…' she said, knowing the quote. 'I…can't speak from experience about marriage. I'm sorry about all that's happened to you. It's not easy being a single parent. Sometimes I feel as though I'm losing my sanity myself, with all the angst. And they aren't even my own children…'

Was his son ill, on top of everything else? She pondered that silently.

'You've been very kind in listening to me,' she added. 'You obviously have your own problems.'

'Who doesn't?' he said. 'I don't trust love, except the love for my son.' Again, he made that last remark almost inaudibly, as though he were talking to himself. It sounded so sad that she felt impulsively that she wanted to reach out and touch his face. Instead, she stared straight ahead, her hands cupped around the warm coffee, concentrating on raindrops hitting the road.

'What else do you trust?' she asked tentatively, after a moment of silence in which she was aware of her heart beating deeply.

'I trust in a spark of goodness in the human spirit,' he said softly. 'I believe in cultivating that, of recognizing it where I find it…and being thankful.'

Deirdre bit her lower lip, wanting to cry. 'Surely that's part of love,' she protested mildly.

'Not that insane sort of love that a man can feel for a woman, and then she lets him down…or vice versa. It's a sort of madness.'

'I think perhaps you're talking about passion,' she said, overcoming her nervousness by a supreme effort, while feeling a stab of something that was, she thought, jealousy for the unknown woman or women for whom he had felt that insane love. 'It's a kind of insanity. That's why the French have a category of crime called *le crime passionel,* which is looked upon leniently because the law recognizes the temporary insanity when such strong emotions are involved. Hopefully, one can also feel a more gentle love as well as the insanity of passion for the same person sometimes.'

'Maybe.' He turned to look at her. 'How do you know all that?' he said.

They were standing very close, and he leaned forward and put a warm hand on her cold cheek, making her face tingle. 'You're cold,' he murmured.

'It's purely theoretical with me—love,' she said hastily, intensely aware of his warm hand yet, oddly, accepting it as quite normal between them, even though they scarcely knew each other. 'I imagine that passion is a very rare emotion. I've never really loved anyone…a man, that is. I love the children.'

It seemed incongruous that she should be saying those things to this man, yet it seemed to come naturally. Unlike many people, he was easy to talk to. She felt he would not judge her.

'You're very sweet,' he said, stroking his thumb very delicately over her cool skin, and for a moment she held her breath at the sheer pleasure of such an unexpected touch, before he dropped his hand.

'That makes me sound very bland,' she said. 'I hope I'm not that.'

'No.'

The desire to put her arms up around his neck, in full view of the comings and goings of the hospital entrance, was so strong that she forced herself to concentrate on not doing it.

'Will you come, then?' he said. 'To dinner, I mean?'

'Yes,' she said.

'Could I call you this evening to set it up?'

'Yes,' she said. 'But, please, don't say that if you've no real intention of following through because, you see, I don't trust either sometimes.'

'I may be a twenty-four-seven man,' he said ruefully, 'but I do keep my word.'

'All right,' she said, looking up at him, wanting so much to kiss him that she felt weak with the effort of holding back. At the same time, she felt as though she were standing back, looking at herself, surprised at herself.

It was crazy, she knew that, because she didn't really know him. Being with him felt right...but, then, she knew that feeling could not always be trusted, especially when you hadn't known a person for very long. Nonetheless, she trusted her own judgement, her own gut feeling. That was all right, so long as you didn't break your own rules for personal safety and personal common sense.

'I must get back to work,' he said, leaning forward quickly to kiss her on the cheek. The brief touch of his warm lips on her cool cheek sent tingles through her.

When he drew back from her they looked at each other for a long moment, as though they could not understand what had happened between them. 'I'm glad I almost ran you down,' he said, taking a step back, away from her. 'Take care.'

Quickly he was gone, striding away from her, back into the hospital, with one backward glance.

'So am I,' she whispered. 'So am I.'

Soon she would walk back to her parents' home for a while, her own home. For the next few moments she would stay here and let this sink in, that it was not a dream that she had met Dr Shay Melburne. There was a feeling of being punch-drunk from the shock of having her life taking a new turn at such short notice, particularly when she had, such a short time ago, been in despair.

She leaned against the wall, facing away from the hospital entrance, and drank what was left of the almost cold coffee, needing to give herself time to think. Before going home she would go into the human resources department and get a job application form. Once she had it in her possession she would take her time over filling it in. She would do the sensible thing, would work out to her own satisfaction, and that of the people who depended on her, how she was going to be able to work part time and be a mother to two children as well. Perhaps after working part time for a few months, to see how it would go, she could consider increasing her hours.

It was obvious to her now that she should have sought counselling when she had lost her job, because it had been a shock, a great anxiety, as well as a blow to her self-confidence and esteem. At the time, her father had not been well and had had to undergo the operation for the removal of part of his gut, so she had thrown herself into helping her parents. Although it had taken her mind off her own dilemma, nothing had been resolved for her as an individual. Then, having the need to earn money, she had taken the job caring for Mungo and Fleur. Maybe it was now time to seek that belated counselling. It would be a great relief to talk to someone, as she had unburdened herself to Shay, to get some feedback.

Yes, something was wrong indeed with her mental equilibrium—even just admitting it brought a certain relief. But somehow she was now beginning to differentiate between the wood and the trees.

CHAPTER FOUR

SLOWLY Deirdre walked to her parents' house, hardly aware of the drizzle that misted her hair. There was so much to think about, yet this time she was very careful to look both ways before she crossed a street.

Maybe she needed to see a psychiatrist, she speculated soberly, still thinking about the counselling, before she should contemplate going to work in a hospital. She had had two major losses in her life at the same time: the loss of her job and then the loss of her parents when they had left the country. Although they would be back before too long, sometimes it seemed as though they were gone for ever, and she mourned them. The stress of loss was the greatest that one had to bear.

Even though her mood had lifted after meeting Shay, blurting out her troubles to him, she could not be sure that the more upbeat mood would last if he were to pull back out of her life. After all, she couldn't say that he was really in her life. No doubt he felt guilty at having almost run her down. At the time, she had taken all the blame without question, or felt she had. He had kissed her on the cheek, but so what? A lot of people kissed, and it seemed to mean nothing to them, a sort of affectation to which she did not subscribe herself. To her, a kiss did mean something special. So her mind chattered, her thoughts moving back and forth, this way and that.

Often when she came near to her own house she had the irrational hope that her parents would be there, that one of them would open the door and give her a hug. Even though they phoned her often, sent e-mails and regular mail frequently, she never stopped missing them—it was not the same as seeing someone. If they had been there, all this angst with her job would have been easier to bear, because she would have had two wise people to talk to, apart from Fiona. She had some friends, of course, but since she had left nursing they had dispersed somewhat and did not meet as frequently. It was also difficult to go out in the evenings when you had children to take care of. Granny McGregor had done a lot of childminding, of course, but somehow she, Deirdre, had felt responsible. Gradually you could find yourself socially isolated.

There was someone to greet her at the house; Mollykins, their ginger, black and white cat who queened it over the house, came and went through a cat flap during the day, on most days. It meant that she, Deirdre, had to visit the house frequently when she wasn't sleeping there, to open and close the cat flap as she could not let the cat out at night. There were coyotes at large that ate cats, that lived in the forested areas and came out in the evenings into the built-up areas.

'Hello, Mollykins,' she crooned to the cat, who came forward quickly to brush against her legs, as though she had been waiting in the hall, knowing the exact moment when Deirdre would come. Deirdre squatted down amongst the letters that had been put through the letter-box and were on the hall mat to stroke the purring Mollykins. No doubt the cat missed her parents as much as she did.

Then she went through the letters, gratified to see that there were two from her parents.

She opened the back door to let the cat out, then opened up the cat flap. What another momentous day it had been, starting with the words she had had with Granny McGregor, then the interesting interlude at the Stanton Memorial. Now she found herself somewhat flustered, not knowing what to do first, her mind filled with the image of Shay. In her own mind she was beginning to accept that she could refer to him by his first name, yet she dared not presume that there would be a relationship between them. The kiss he had given her on the cheek had been a kiss of commiseration at her predicament, she felt sure. Even so, it was a relief that he was not married. That didn't mean that he had no other women in his life, though.

She flung her coat on a chair in the hall and went into the kitchen to make tea, going through the motions to calm her thoughts, which seemed to be all over the place. Sipping tea a few moments later, she was standing in the middle of the kitchen and staring out through the window at the rain-sodden late autumn garden when the main telephone rang.

'Hi, Dee. Just calling to find out where you are,' Mungo's voice announced when she picked up the kitchen extension. 'Are we having supper at your place tonight?' Deirdre knew him well enough to recognize a certain timbre of anxiety in his tone, and her heart softened with love for him. Maybe he needed to reassure himself that she was still in his life and would remain there. He was very masculine, yet gentle at the same time, not feeling the need to be aggressive to prove that he was one hundred per cent male, as so many boys and men did. Some men never outgrew that need to prove themselves, it seemed to her, and it could be tedious for those who had to deal with them.

'Would you like to?' she said. 'I thought maybe we would. I've got food here.'

'Yeah,' he said. 'I'd like to sleep over there, too. I need to get away from Jerry for a bit.'

'That's fine with me. Will you tell Fleur?'

'Sure. Be there about the usual time,' he said, his voice brightening, as though a load had been lifted off his shoulders.

Mungo went to a high school within easy walking distance of the house, and Fleur's school, the middle school, was fortunately on the same campus. Mungo and Fleur came home together, having a designated spot where they met up each day. Sometimes Deirdre drove them, when her ancient car was in good working order, and if Mungo was sick, she always came and went to school with Fleur. She never took any chances with their safety.

Deirdre was left with the task of letting Jerry know that they would be spending the night at her house, something which he didn't generally mind about, as it meant zero responsibility for him, and she suspected that he had a woman there, discreetly, when no one else was there. For most of the time he wanted to present himself as a grieving widower—at least he was contesting Moira's last wishes. It was a relief that he did not answer the phone, so that she could leave a voice-mail message.

When the telephone shrilled again a few moments later she thought it might be him, angry at her again for some reason, so she answered warily.

'Hello, Deirdre.' It was Shay. 'I thought I would give you a call to see if you had had time to get to the human resources department. If not, maybe I could go there for you.'

'That's kind of you,' she said, glad that he could not see her flush of pleasure, although no doubt he could hear that pleasure in her voice. She had given him the telephone numbers of the two houses, as well as her mobile phone number. 'But I did manage to get one. I thought I would wait a while before actually applying…to sort things out first. Thank you again for your time today.'

'My pleasure,' he said. 'Let me know if I can be of any further help.' Deirdre wondered whether he felt sorry for her, could see that she desperately needed help. Somehow it didn't matter so long as she could sustain some sort of contact with him. There was a pause, as though he didn't want to hang up, and she didn't know what to say next. Then the thought came to her that perhaps this was his way of saying goodbye, having salved his conscience by being of some help to her—even though he had asked her out to dinner.

'If you're not doing anything this evening, Dr Melburne,' she said in a rush, 'perhaps you would like to come over here to eat with me and the two children, about seven, or earlier?' She gave him the address hurriedly, before she lost her nerve.

'I'll come on one condition,' he said, amusement in his voice, 'that you stop calling me Dr Melburne.'

'All right…Shay,' she said.

'That's better,' he said. 'I'll be there as soon as I can, after I've done rounds. If I'm going to be more than a few minutes late, I'll call you.'

'All right. See you then,' she said, thinking it would be interesting to see if he was really late, if he were still 'the twenty-four-seven man' that this former wife had accused him of being. Deirdre tried to picture her face, the mysterious Antonia, and failed. The name sounded glamorous to her and she was curious to know what sort of woman had captivated the very attractive and sophisticated Shay Melburne.

There was a lot to be done. She rushed around tidying the house, which was already perfectly clean but had that unlived-in air. They could have a seafood stir-fry for supper, with fresh vegetables, so she took out some frozen prawns and scallops from the freezer to thaw under cold water. Quickly she set the table in the small dining room near the kitchen, then put on the gas heater in that room. It looked like an old-fashioned cast-iron wood stove, with real flames. By candlelight it looked good at this time of the year. In the sitting room she did the same, putting on lamps. Although the house was small, somewhat humble and unpretentious, she often thought, it was nicely and tastefully furnished.

In the bathroom she brushed her hair and put on a little make-up, contemplating her pale face and somewhat haunted eyes, which had dark shadows under them. She could not really call herself pretty, or beautiful, yet she had an interesting face, with regular features; a man she had liked a lot had once called her face 'arresting'. Thinking of that now, she smiled at her reflection as she smeared a little green eye shadow on her lids. 'Vanity, thy name is woman,' she said aloud to her reflection. 'One of the lesser vices.'

The beds for Fleur and Mungo were already made up in the small, single-storey-plus-basement house, which had three bedrooms. They kept some of their clothes and other personal belongings there, too. She changed into a wool skirt and a lightweight sweater.

Mungo and Fleur came first, as she knew they would, lugging their knapsacks of homework books.

'We're eating in the dining room,' she announced, 'because Dr Melburne's coming to supper. And in case you're wondering, he's divorced. He told me that himself today.'

'Well, that's better than if he was married,' Mungo said, ever practical, 'if you really like him, Dee.'

'I do like him,' she said. 'But really we don't know each other that well...'

'Ooh, that's nice,' Fleur said, standing in the doorway of the dining room, looking in. 'It's really warm and cosy.'

'Great!' Mungo chipped in, as they both lugged their heavy

bags into the living room. 'Can we watch television for a bit, Dee?' Their favourite programme was on.

'OK,' she said, 'but then you have to help me serve the supper, and then get on with your homework. I don't suppose Dr Melburne will stay long, he's a busy man.'

'I really like him,' Fleur said. 'Are you going to marry him, Dee?'

'Goodness, no!' she said, knowing that she was protesting too much and repeating herself. 'I've only known him for…well, a relatively short time.'

'So long as he doesn't take you away from us,' Mungo said. They were both very astute, and could probably tell a lot from her flushed face. 'Is there any juice, Dee?'

'Yes, help yourself.'

When Shay came she was in a state of nerves, especially as he was fifteen minutes later than she had expected. The food, which had been easy to cook, was ready. She had decided not to open a bottle of wine, not wanting him to think that she was making a special effort for him. She let Mungo go to the door to let him in while she lit candles in the cosy small dining room where the flames from the lighted gas in the simulated log fire flickered enticingly. The three of them often ate their supper in the dining room instead of at the kitchen table, and always when Granny McGregor joined them or any other guests.

'Let me take your coat,' Fleur said to Shay politely.

'Thank you.'

When Deirdre came out into the hall, he handed her a small bunch of flowers. 'Winter pansies,' he said. 'I'm a little late, so I hope you're not starving.'

'They're lovely,' she said, looking at the velvety flowers, some of deep purple, some yellow. 'We're just about to serve the food. You won't mind if we eat right away? There's homework to be done.'

'No, that's great.'

'I'll just put the flowers in water. Mungo, please, show Dr Melburne where he can wash his hands, then the dining room. I'll be with you in a few minutes.'

He looked pale and tired, she thought, the way she used to look after a day in the operating suite sometimes. He was wearing the black turtleneck sweater under his overcoat, simple and sophisticated.

As she put the pansies into a vase, then put them on a small table in the front hall, she found that her hands were shaking. Quickly she went into the bathroom and splashed cold water on her face. It was suddenly very important that Shay should like her, but the last thing she wanted was for it to be obvious, either to him or to the children.

When she brought the food into the dining room, she found the three of them sitting at the table, with Mungo playing the part of host, rather as though he were in a play, one of the parts he liked to play in the school drama class. Deirdre stifled a smile. She always tried hard to give the children certain social graces that would be useful to them now and in later life. Mainly, she included them in everything and made them contribute their share to whatever event was taking place in the home. She thought she was succeeding. For the most part, they were well mannered, polite and reasonably competent in all social situations.

In short order, she was seated with them at the table, with serving dishes of steaming food in front of them. There was jasmine rice to go with the seafood and vegetables.

'This is great,' Shay said. 'Thank you for inviting me.'

Deirdre began to pass the dishes around. 'There's a fruit salad for dessert,' she said, happiness rising in her like a tide. It was a rare occurrence these days for her to have a guest to dinner. Most of the time she cooked for Jerry's guests, but did not join them for the meal. Here, in her own home, she was in charge. Very quickly they were chatting, laughing and eating as though they had known Shay for a long time.

'Where is your son tonight?' Mungo said boldly, after a while, to Shay. 'We could have invited him, too. Or is he at boarding school?'

Shay hesitated, his knife and fork poised over his plate, and Deirdre was conscious of holding her breath, looking down at her plate. 'He's not at boarding school, but he is away at the moment for a week or two. Normally he lives with me and I'm sure he would enjoy a meal like this. Next time, perhaps, if there is a next time…if you're good enough to invite me again.'

'What school does he go to?' Mungo asked.

'St Andrew's College,' Shay replied, naming a prestigious private boys' school in Prospect Bay.

'We play soccer sometimes against them,' Mungo said eagerly. 'I really like soccer.'

'Maybe you've met, then,' Shay said. 'Mark plays soccer.'

There were vibes that she could not understand, and Deirdre covered up quickly. 'We'll make sure there is a next time for supper,' she said lightly. 'You'll have to let us know when it would be a good time.'

'I will,' he said quietly, looking at her over the tops of the two flickering candles, down the length of the small dining table where they sat opposite each other.

Deirdre smiled at him, knowing that they had common ground there in the care of children. If his son was sick and he wanted her to know about it, he would tell her in his own time.

Music was playing softly from the radio in the kitchen and the atmosphere became very relaxed as they talked about films they had seen and concerts they had been to. Shay knew exactly what would interest the children. It was sad that his marriage hadn't lasted but, then, if it had, he would not be here with her…

When they had finished eating, Fleur and Mungo went into the sitting room to tackle their homework, spreading their books out on the coffee-table, the sofa and the floor, while Deirdre and Shay cleared the table.

'I expect you have to hurry away,' she said shyly as they stood in the kitchen, having carried out the last of the dishes and plates.

'Soon,' he said, glancing at the kitchen clock. 'That was a great meal, Deirdre. Thank you.'

'I'm glad you could come,' she said, her spirits soaring. Yes, it had been a good meal.

'I must have sounded rather secretive about my son,' he said slowly, keeping his voice low. 'Well…he's been in a rehabilitation hospital for a week. He inadvertently took an overdose of a drug. For some time he's had a drug problem…which started with smoking pot. It's been a bit of a nightmare for both of us, not least for me because I feel guilty about the divorce, to say the least. He's desperate to get out of it now, but he'll be in the hospital for at least another week.'

Deirdre stopped what she was doing, her hands hovering over the dirty dishes. 'I'm so sorry to hear that,' she said quietly. 'He didn't…um…try…?'

'No,' he finished for her, 'he didn't try to kill himself. He's assured me of that, and I believe him. Not just because I want to believe him. He got in with a bad crowd, which is often what happens when you don't spend enough time with your children and don't show them the affection they need, even when you love them more than anything on earth.' He began to pace up and down, his hands in his trouser pockets. 'They have to know it themselves, they have to see it—and not just in things that you buy for them, material things making up for the lack of time. I don't believe in "quality time", that rather idiotic catch-phrase that is designed to make neglectful parents feel good. Time is time. That's what children see. Sometimes they just want you in the same room, whether you're interacting with them or not, just sitting reading a newspaper, knowing that you're with them because you want to be there more than anything else. The same applies to a spouse, of course.'

'Yes,' she answered him feelingly, a sober sense of recognition enabling her to understand only too well what he was saying. It was clear to her then that he needed, in his own way, to talk to someone as desperately as she needed to. 'That must be very difficult to deal with…the drug issue. It's something I absolutely dread. I pray that I will never need to. You try at all times to know who they're with, what they're doing. It's not easy…'

'No, it isn't.' He stood leaning against the kitchen wall, seemingly casual, yet she could feel the tension in him.

'How did he start into it?' she asked.

'The usual thing. Experimenting with smoking pot at school—not wanting to be the odd one out when others were doing it, then getting hooked. It was at the time when he was under a lot of stress because of his mother's departure. For quite a while I suspected that something was up, but I could never prove it. And he denied it, as I guess he would. He wasn't proud of it. He later took pills, hence the overdose.'

'It seems so easy for them to get drugs,' she said, fear in her heart that she might have to deal with what he was now tackling.

'It is. Finally, the school caught several of the boys smoking pot on school property and they were threatened with suspension and expulsion. To cut a long story short, the school decided to give them counselling and a second chance. Things seem to be more under control there now, going in the right direction. It's what goes on outside school property that's more difficult to deal with.'

'You must be very relieved at the attitude the school is taking,' she said feelingly, abandoning any attempt to clear up while he was there. It could all wait. 'Would you like a cup of coffee?' she offered. 'You've made me see that my own problems are not so difficult to deal with after all. With me, it's mainly getting up the courage to make changes…once I can see my way clear.'

'Aye, there's the rub,' he said, with a rueful laugh. 'Seeing your way clear says a lot. There's not a person on this earth who doesn't have something to contend with, Deirdre. I see tragic things every day in my job that require a great deal of courage to face up to for the patients. I think my part is difficult, just telling them. We feel so alone because we often don't even suspect about others' problems until we open up ourselves, then other people start talking. Even so, we still have to deal with our own problems, we just feel a bit less isolated when we can talk.' As he spoke, he walked around the small kitchen, looking at things—the drawings on the fridge door, the pictures on the walls, the potted plants.

'Yes…' Deirdre stood by the table, looking at him. She wanted to go into his arms, to feel them close around her, to put her head against his shoulder and close her eyes, feel the warmth of his body against hers, knowing that he was deriving comfort from her also. When she had first set eyes on him he had seemed so in command, and she had been so full of her own angst that the idea that he might be human in that way had not entered her head.

'As one of my patients said to me recently when I broke the news to her that she had cancer,' he went on, staring thoughtfully at Deirdre from the other side of the kitchen table, 'it didn't help her to know that I might get knocked down and killed by a truck while crossing a street long before she died of cancer. She still had to deal with her cancer. What she wanted, more than anything, was the wisdom and company of other women who had the same kind of cancer that she had. That would really help her. Some doctors actually say to their patients, "Oh, I might get knocked down by a truck tomorrow," but it's meaningless, because they don't really believe it, they don't feel their mortality tapping them on the shoulder.'

'No,' Deirdre agreed. 'I would call that a serious lack of a bedside manner. But, then, people in the medical and nursing profession don't talk much about that now, so I find. When I was training, they did still talk about it.'

The electric clock on the wall ticked loudly as they stood and looked at each other. There was a tension of recognition between them, on so many levels. If only she could hug him…

'If…if there's any way at all that I can help you…with your son, I would be happy if you would let me know. I don't want to presume.'

'Thank you,' he said, his eyes locking with hers, intense and tired. 'You've done a lot for me already, Deirdre, without even trying.'

Oh, I'm trying, she thought. Believe me, I'm trying.

'I will have that coffee, please, just a very small one, otherwise I'll have no hope of sleeping tonight,' he said, making a visible attempt to lighten the atmosphere. 'Then I really have to go, reluctantly. It's been a very pleasant interlude. If I hadn't felt so relaxed after that great dinner, I wouldn't have been able to tell you about Mark. Usually I feel pretty uptight about it. I get the impression that you can keep a confidence, that you don't gossip.'

Deirdre nodded. 'Does his mother know?' she asked, getting the coffee things ready. Since he had already told her so much, she sensed that she could now ask certain things.

'Not yet. There's no point in worrying her when she's a long way away. And he said he didn't want her to know. I will probably tell her when he's completely rehabilitated, because he would like to see her. He feels bitter that she left him...not so much that she left me but that she discarded him, as he sees it. I don't suppose it was easy for her either, she wanted custody. But Mark didn't like the guy she was with—there was no way he could call him Dad and go to live away from here. I wanted him, too.'

'There's an open invitation to you and your son,' she said, pouring boiling water over coffee grains, wishing she could say more. 'Here, to my parents' house. Just let us know.' Her intuition told her that he was informing her quite clearly that he had feet of clay, because he sensed that she was interested in him as a man. He was being honest with her, perhaps asking her to stand back until she knew what he was all about. For that, she respected him.

'I will. Thanks.' He took the coffee that she handed him.

'Thanks to you, Shay,' she said sincerely. 'You've given me hope of getting a job in nursing. Not so long ago I was in despair.'

He looked at her ruefully. 'I haven't done such a good job with my son,' he said.

'It's not possible to police everything they do,' she said.

'If I hadn't been working so much, maybe I would have noticed sooner that things were not right,' he said. 'I have a housekeeper, and she alerted me, but I can't expect her to be a mother to my son. She has her own family and private life.'

Deirdre poured a very small cup of coffee for herself, knowing it might keep her awake. That would make a change from anxiety keeping her awake, she mused. Somehow she knew that any sleeplessness she experienced tonight would be of a different quality.

As they sipped coffee, they could hear Mungo and Fleur discussing something. It felt like a peaceful domestic scene, and Deirdre felt a rare contentment, in spite of the shadow that seemed to hang over them from the revelations that Shay had just made.

'At the schools the kids go to, they're very mindful of the drug scene,' she said. 'There are all sorts of measures in place. It's all brought out into the open, so that we're aware of what could happen. A child can be suspended on the spot, the parents called to remove him or her from the school right away. It's talked about at assembly frequently. It's the same thing with bullying. They have zero tolerance for bullying.'

'That's good,' he said. 'So that you don't think it could never happen to you.'

'What you've said has certainly put my problems into perspective,' she said again.

When it was time for him to leave, he said goodbye to the children and Deirdre went with him to the door, where he put on his overcoat. As she opened the door, he took her arm and guided her outside, pulling the door closed behind them. 'Thanks again,' he said. 'If you need someone to talk to, just call me any time. I have plenty of people I can talk to at the hospital about my own problems. Otherwise, I'll be in touch about going out to dinner.'

'Yes.' The word came out in a whisper, as she wished that he did not have to go.

'I may not be much good at giving advice,' he said, 'but I can listen, and maybe suggest a different angle on things. I've made a bit of a mess of my life.'

'Don't say that,' she said. 'I'm sure you're a great doctor and surgeon.' Judging by the way his colleagues had responded to him during the tour of the operating suite, he was very respected and liked at the hospital.

'At the expense of just about everything else,' he said. 'I can't set myself up as an example. I have to remind myself that what I'm doing is a job, it isn't my whole life, it isn't who I am. One day it's going to come to an end. Goodnight, Deirdre.'

They stood looking at each other in the dim light of the streetlamps, reluctant to make a move away. 'I…' she said. Then she found herself reaching forward and putting her hands on his shoulders, feeling an overwhelming empathy with him about his son, away somewhere in a hospital. The attraction that she felt moved her. 'Shay…I…'

With a muffled groan he put his hands on her waist and pulled her against him, hard against his body, and she put her face up for his kiss. His lips were firm and demanding on hers, yet gentle at the same time, and she closed her eyes, the pleasure of his mouth on hers like a long-remembered dream.

He put up one hand to hold her head against his, his fingers in her hair, as his mouth moved warmly, sensually on hers. Pressed hard against him, Deirdre put her hand up into his hair, holding him as he was holding her, wanting the kiss to go on for ever. Unfamiliar sensations, like fingers of fire, moved through her body, and she knew that she wanted him as much as he obviously wanted her. Once again, she knew that she was in danger of falling in love with Dr Shay Melburne.

They pulled back simultaneously, breathing quickly. 'Goodnight,' she whispered.

'Goodnight,' he said. 'I'll see you very soon.'

'Yes…please,' she murmured.

Then he kissed her again quickly, crushing her mouth with his, holding her tightly as though he didn't want her to go, any more than she wanted him to go.

'Dee! Dee! Where are you?' Fleur's imperious voice called from the hallway behind them, and Shay pulled back, stepping away from her, running his hands down the length of her arms and gripping her hands hard, before letting go.

Abruptly he turned away from her and strode to the garden gate and to his car parked outside. He raised a hand to her in silent farewell, while she wanted to call out to him not to go.

'Dee!'

Deirdre went inside, feeling dazed by the speed of events and the shock of learning about Shay's son. That knowledge had had a sobering effect on her, made her own concerns seem almost petty. 'Here I am,' she called. 'Just seeing Dr Melburne out.'

'Can you help me with something, Dee?' Fleur said. 'I've got to learn a poem. Can you listen to see if I've got it right?'

'Sure,' she said, contented that Fleur needed her.

'You know, I really like Dr Melburne,' Fleur volunteered. 'He's sort of…genuine, you know? Real cool.'

'I know what you mean,' Deirdre said.

'Is he going to be your boyfriend?'

'I don't know right now,' Deirdre said with a laugh. 'I sure would like him to be my boyfriend. Anything else you would like to know?'

'Not right now,' Fleur answered pertly. 'I've got other things on my mind.'

'Just as well.'

Deirdre followed Fleur into the sitting room to help with the homework. It had been a long, tiring day, and she was glad that they were all sleeping here in her house. The room looked very lived in and homely, with scattered books and papers, the fire flickering. Not for the first time, she felt deep gratitude for having this house. Not least in her gratitude was the stability of the life that her parents had given her while she had been growing up. Before too long they would be back in the country, then probably her brother would be back, too, when his contract in Australia had expired. They were a close-knit family, she realized more and more, with a strong emotional bond.

She was also realizing more than ever that there was probably no way that she could work anything other than part time in a job as demanding as operating room work—at least, not for quite some time, especially as one had to be on the job by seven o'clock in the morning, or just after, to start the operating list at eight o'clock sharp.

Tomorrow she would go over the application forms, fill them in and get her résumé in order, but would not actually apply until other things had been sorted out. There would be the issue of getting the children to school. Even though they were old enough to get themselves there, she knew the dangers of leaving children to fend for themselves, of putting them in a position where they felt neglected, unsupervised, unloved. Even though Mungo was in his teens and Fleur would soon be there, she could not suppose that they were more sophisticated than they actually were, because it was convenient for her to do so.

She would also make an appointment with her GP to get the name of a counsellor for herself—that was the top priority. With the other things, there was no need to rush. It all had to be just right. What had happened over the past little while had frightened her, the spiral down into a depression, into a kind of helplessness.

Fiona wanted her to be the legal guardian of the children in the event of her, Fiona's, demise, so they would have to go to see Fiona's lawyer very soon to look into it. She rather dreaded that. She was coming round to the idea that she could never abandon the children. Shay's story had left her with a feeling now almost like a physical sickness, an apprehension about what could happen to children who thought they had been abandoned by a parent, as indeed Mark had been by his mother. Not the least of her worries was the certainty of the fury that Jerry would be in when he knew the full extent of Fiona's plans. There was no doubt that he would fight tooth and nail to prevent Fiona's wishes from becoming a reality.

'Here's the poem,' Fleur said, handing her a computer print-out. 'It's Scottish.'

'Oh, heck,' she said, laughing. 'I hope you don't have to do the authentic Scottish accent, because I won't know what you're saying.'

'Naw,' Fleur said. 'Dinna fash yourself…or whatever.'

'I used to know this poem myself, believe it or not. Sit down there,' she said, indicating the sofa, 'and say on.' She lowered herself to the floor at Fleur's feet, the rest of the sofa being taken up with books. Mungo gave them a resigned glance, no doubt having had to listen to this recitation before.

Deirdre grinned at him. Tonight she would get some sleep, and no doubt have pleasant dreams. The reality of those kisses would be like balm to her soul.

Later, when Fleur and Mungo were in bed, she cleared up the kitchen and stacked the dishwasher, a quiet time so that she could think. Only the cat stalked around the kitchen to keep her company.

You got frightened when you thought that your mind might have become fragile, when you felt you were at breaking point and did not know where to go from there. Not too long ago she had felt like that, somehow on the edge of something, where she might fall over the edge and had no idea how to stop herself. It was all the more frightening because she had always thought of herself as strong, someone who could be strong for herself and for other people as well.

Now she understood that it was time to look after herself, to find out what it was that she needed and work out how she might get it. If she were to go back to outside work, three days a week, say, she would have to elicit Fiona's help to supervise the children's journey to school on those days. Fiona still drove a car, her health appeared good in that regard, so she could drive them. The kids would have to sleep at whichever house was the most convenient the night before each working day. That meant disruption for them, but not so much as having Deirdre out of their lives altogether.

She sighed as she put out the light and went up the stairs. Something would be worked out.

CHAPTER FIVE

'THE week before Christmas is a good time to start your orientation. We've just had a bout of activity in surgery as the surgeons finished their pending cases, and now they want to relax in the run-up to Christmas,' Darlene Reade, the head nurse of the operating suite, said to Deirdre as they stood in the main corridor just outside the head nurse's office. 'Of course, we'll have emergencies—road-traffic accidents and everything else.'

Deirdre nodded. 'Yes,' she agreed. A feeling that she recognized as elation, something rare, seemed to flood over her as she stood there in the familiar surroundings of an operating suite, with the familiar sights and smells, the scent of cleanness.

There were four of them standing there on a Monday morning, three newly employed registered nurses who were about to undergo a three-week orientation period and the head nurse who was about to hand them over to a tutor for the department who would help them with the actual orientation. To Deirdre's surprise and gratitude, there was such a shortage of experienced operating room nurses that the head nurse had agreed to let her do her orientation part time, and had given her the days that she wanted to work—Mondays, Wednesdays and Fridays. The fact that these were Shay's operating days had had something to do with her request.

A middle-aged woman came up to them and introduced herself. 'Hi, I'm Caroline Clarke,' she said, extending a hand to each. 'Now, you're Deirdre Warwick.' She peered at Deirdre's ID badge which had her photograph on it, pinned to the top pocket of a white lab coat that she wore over a blue scrub suit. 'And this is Suzy Jacobs, and you are Beth Strom. Right?'

They all shook hands with her. The three new nurses had introduced themselves in the locker room earlier.

'I'll leave you now,' the head nurse said, taking her departure.

'First of all, I'll show you around the place,' the tutor said. 'I know you've each been shown around at least once before, but this time we are going to poke into cupboards. I'm going to show you where we keep the emergency instrument trays, like the tracheostomy set, where we keep the defibrillator, the cardiac arrest drugs, the crash cart, and all that sort of stuff. We're going to look in every cupboard and every drawer. As far as possible, we try to keep each actual operating room identical with the next one, although there are specialized rooms that have extras, of course. Got your notebooks and pens, everyone?'

'Yes,' they chorused.

'Right. Off we go, then. We'll go to the stockroom first.'

The main corridor of the operating suite was busy, in a controlled way, with the comings of patients on stretchers for the first operation of the day, pushed by porters, to be parked outside the rooms where they were to be operated on. There were fifteen operating rooms in Stanton Memorial Hospital, which was quite a lot for a relatively small hospital. The time was twenty minutes to eight.

Deirdre looked around her quickly at the busy scene, all carefully organized and choreographed, like a dance. Half her mind was on what Fleur and Mungo would be doing—being given breakfast by Granny McGregor and gathering together their stuff for school at Jerry's house. Jerry himself had left on another business trip, thank goodness. He was to be in Hong Kong and China for several weeks, including over Christmas. Deirdre suspected that he had a female travelling companion, which she didn't want to know about. It was none of her business, anyway. It was just great that he wasn't around.

She felt somewhat disorientated, but in a good way, as though she could hardly believe her luck—not in the strange way that had come upon her suddenly when she had been unable to get off the bus. She felt that she needed to tell herself frequently that this was really happening. Sometimes something good did come out of trouble after all, especially when one found the courage from somewhere to ask for help.

They stood in the large stockroom, looking at the shelves of supplies that they would need every day in the operating rooms, from hypodermic syringes to plastic chest tubes, bladder catheters, latex surgical gloves and dressings, to name but a few.

Yes, it was good to be back.

'Hello, Caroline,' a familiar voice said from the doorway, and Deirdre turned quickly to see Shay standing there in his surgical scrubs, looking very attractive. Her heart leapt in recognition as she strove to keep her delight off her face.

'Hi, Shay,' the tutor greeted him. 'Meet three new RNs, just starting orientation today. They're all experienced in OR work.'

Grinning, he came forward to shake hands, leaving Deirdre to the last. 'I know Ms Warwick,' he said. 'Our paths have crossed.'

'That's good,' the tutor remarked, 'because she could be working with you later on today. Or maybe just observing.'

'Throwing them in at the deep end, huh?' he said.

'That's my style,' she replied.

'See you all later, then,' he said, smiling at Deirdre, while the other two RNs looked at her.

'How did you meet him?' one of them whispered to her later when they had moved on out of the stockroom.

'Not in the usual way,' she said, laughing. 'He almost ran me down with his car.'

'I wouldn't mind him running me down.'

The place became very hectic for a while until those first patients had been wheeled into their respective operating rooms from the main corridor. For the duration of those operations, both long and short, there would be relative quiet in the corridor, until the porters wheeled in the next patients from the wards or the holding areas. Some of the patients were from the day-stay unit, who would only be in the hospital for one day or maybe overnight.

Just before lunch, the three nurses on orientation found themselves assigned to a different operating room each, for the purposes of observation. As she had hoped and expected, Deirdre found herself in operating room one where Shay was operating on a patient who was having a gut resection for cancer of the colon. She had ascertained that by looking at the posted list outside before entering the room.

As Deirdre stood in the background, a mask on her face, her hair covered with the usual disposable paper mob-cap, she knew that Shay would probably not have time to say much to her, he had to concentrate on what he was doing. There was an assistant surgeon and a resident-in-training with him, scrubbed up to help him with the case. That made four in the sterile field by the patient, including the scrub nurse. An anaesthetist stood at the patient's head.

Deirdre felt excited, interested and somewhat stressed, trying to take it all in, not wanting to miss anything. Yes, she told herself again, it was good to be back in the familiar surroundings of an operating suite, yet she had got out of the way of being constantly alert, constantly on the ball, as it were. No doubt that would come back very quickly as her confidence rose. That was partly what the orientation period was intended to accomplish. For now, she stood silently watching, careful to keep out of the path of the circulating nurse, the RN who was in charge of the room and who was running everything outside the sterile field.

Another thing that she had lost the knack of was being able to close her mind to her own life outside the hospital. A lot of the time she was thinking of Fleur and Mungo, wondering what they were doing, even though she knew the routines of their days in detail. For the first time since taking the job of looking after them, she had not been able to carry a cellphone with her to be available constantly. They knew the number of the department and would be able to find her in a few minutes, but it was not the same as having her own telephone in her pocket. It wasn't as though they were really young, she told herself, and needed her constantly.

With a conscious mental effort she dragged her mind away from the domestic scene. She had, of course, known that the transition would not be instant; neither had she expected to be torn in two with quite so much angst. What she was learning in these first hours, what was being confirmed for her, was that she could never abandon Fleur and Mungo while they needed her. How much worse would it be, she wondered, if they were her own biological children?

Once the piece of gut was removed by Shay and passed to the scrub nurse, who put it into a stainless-steel dish, he turned to Deirdre where she stood behind him, well back, as though he had been fully aware that she had been there all along. 'Hi, Deirdre,' he said. 'Come a little closer. This patient has a car-cinoma of the descending colon and, as you can see, I've removed a large chunk of the gut. Fortunately for him, we've got it in the early stages and it hasn't spread to the omentum or the liver. It has not invaded through the wall of the colon. He should do very well.'

Deirdre nodded. 'That's good,' she said, knowing that the prognosis for cancer of the colon was good if there was no spread. Once in the liver, it was a different story, unless there was one localized lesion, which could then be surgically removed.

As she watched, he took a scalpel and carefully cut open the piece of intestine that he had removed, to reveal the tumour inside the lumen. 'There you have it,' he said. 'Nasty.'

Then he put on a new sterile pair of latex gloves.

'I'm going to staple the two cut ends together,' he said to Deirdre. 'I'm sure you know all about that.'

'Well, I expect you have some new gadgets since I last assisted with a gut resection,' she said. She would just watch what the scrub nurse handed him, then what he did. The circulating nurse brought her a low standing stool so that she could be raised up a few inches and get a better view of what was going on with the operation.

'Thanks,' she said.

Shay turned back to the task in hand and said no more to her for a long time. The room was more or less silent, apart from some exchanged remarks, the muted sound of the anaesthetic equipment and the intermittent sound of the suction equipment. Deirdre forgot herself, even managed to put Fleur and Mungo out of her mind while she concentrated on what was going on in front of her, knowing that she was free to leave the room whenever she wanted to.

There was the usual coffee-lounge in the operating suite for nurses and doctors, just off the main corridor. Already she and the other two nurses on orientation had been there for a coffee-break. The main staff cafeteria for the whole hospital was the one on the ground floor of the building that she had been to with Shay. Then there was the little coffee-shop in the main lobby where she and Shay had bought coffee on her first visit. That seemed like a long time ago. When this case was over she would go to the main cafeteria for lunch, so the tutor had instructed her, then they would all meet up later for a mini-lecture. So far, she was enjoying every minute of it.

Eventually the final instrument and sponge count had been done by the two nurses to make sure that no instruments or gauze sponges had been left inside the patient's abdominal cavity. Shay stripped off his latex rubber gloves and left the suturing of the abdomen to his assistant and the surgical resident.

Beckoning Deirdre over to the side of the room, he proceeded to write notes on the patient's chart about the procedure he had just done, talking to her at the same time.

'Will you be going to the cafeteria for lunch?' he asked.

'Yes,' she said.

'Good. I'll meet you down there in about ten minutes, if you like,' he said.

The others in the room were probably thinking that he was talking to her about the case as he wrote busily, Deirdre concluded. Yes, she would like to meet him.

Deirdre nodded. 'I'll see you there, then,' she said, her heart singing. At the same time she told herself not to read too much into his actions.

'Right. Save me a seat,' he said quietly, looking at her sideways and grinning. At least, his eyes smiled; she could not see the lower part of his face. She was aware that the circulating nurse was looking at her, probably wondering how this new nurse was familiar with the surgeon.

When she went out of the room, she searched for the tutor

to let her know that the operation was over, that she would be leaving for lunch. She would need to put a lab coat over her scrub suit.

Deirdre was part way through her light lunch when Shay came over to her table, carrying a tray with coffee and a sandwich on it.

'Hi, can't stay long,' he said. 'Nice to see you here, Deirdre.' At close proximity he looked pale and tired, but nonetheless very attractive. There were fine lines fanning out from his blue-grey eyes that looked at her with such intensity, and she found that she liked the signs of maturity in him. Parenthood and the demands of his profession obviously took a toll on him, something that she could identify with wholeheartedly.

The twenty-four-seven man, she thought. But, then, that was part of the job—the rushing, watching the clock, being always available. 'Can't be helped,' she said, smiling. 'I'm enjoying being here so far, even if I am a bit disorientated.'

'That's great,' he said. 'I wanted to meet you here to ask what you're doing for Christmas.' He took a bite out of a sandwich.

Since she had invited him to supper at her parents' house, they had been out to dinner once in a restaurant, after which she wondered if that was to be the extent of their friendship as he had not contacted her again. At that time he had informed her that his professional life was hectic, that any free time he had left over he spent with his son, so she had accepted that, thinking she might not see him again outside work. He had paid his dues for almost running her down. Now his query about Christmas made her hope that there might be something else after all.

'We'll be having Christmas dinner at the children's grandmother's house,' she said, thinking of the superb dinners that Fiona produced when she was in the mood to do so.

'Would you and the kids like to come to my place for dinner on Boxing Day?' he asked. 'You don't have to tell me right now if you want to ask them first. My housekeeper's a good cook, but she'll have the day off and Mark and I will do most of the cooking—something simple.'

'I'd like to come. Leftover turkey would be fine,' she said, smiling. 'I expect that Mungo and Fleur would be happy to come.'

'Maybe that's what you'll get, leftover turkey,' he responded. 'I'd really like you to meet Mark, and I've sounded him out about meeting Mungo and Fleur. He seems keen.'

'Is he…is he out of hospital?' she asked hesitantly. 'I know it isn't any of my business, but I felt very…sorry when you told me about him.' She was also wondering too how much Mark missed his mother at Christmas. That was something she could not ask right now.

'Yes. He's going back on an outpatient basis, which seems to be working well for him,' Shay said, as he ate quickly. 'He still needs counselling for the loss of his mother, as well as for the drug thing.'

'Does his mother write to him?' she enquired, unable to resist the question.

'Oh, yes. They write to each other,' he said. 'And unlike the wicked parents one reads about in fact and fiction, I do not confiscate her letters before he can get his hands on them.' Shay smiled ruefully at her. 'I know that happens.'

'I'd certainly like to meet him,' Deirdre said. 'Thank you for the invitation. I'll sound out the children tonight.'

'And the children's stepfather?' he queried.

'He's going to be out of the country over Christmas and New Year. He doesn't like Christmas.'

Shay took a lined card out of his pocket and wrote his home address on it, and simple instructions about how to get there.

'Here,' he said, passing it over to her. 'Not much time now before Christmas. Give me a call, Deirdre.' He chomped on the last of his sandwich and took a swallow of coffee.

'I'll call you tomorrow, if that's all right,' she said.

'Yes. Call me at home. You can leave a message if I'm not in.' He reached across the small table and squeezed her hand briefly as it lay on the top. 'I'd really like you to come,' he said. 'And I'm glad you're working here. Good luck.' He stood up, preparing to leave. 'Bye for now, Deirdre.'

'Thank you,' she said shyly. 'Bye.'

Then he was gone, taking the tray with him, and for a few seconds she had the odd feeling that he had been a figment of her imagination, her wishes and desires. Then she saw him going out. He raised a hand to her as he went out of the main door and she waved back tentatively. She was falling for him, falling in love with him. Was it genuine? she agonized. Or was it just that she was so starved for attention from an attractive, good man? In some ways it frightened her, the growing intensity of her feelings. For a long time she had led a rather circumscribed life, which was not good for anyone. She had needed someone like him, and then suddenly there he had been. The situation was not perfect but, then, what was? They both had difficulties in their lives.

Soon she would be going for a second session with a counsellor, whom she had found through her GP. The counsellor was helping her to sort out her worry about being a mother to someone else's children, of being so emotionally attached to them that she could never treat the relationship like a job from which she could give notice. You could not dice with people's lives in that way, with their emotional needs. She needed help with her depression which had resulted from the impasse she was in.

The counsellor had informed her that she would essentially

cure herself by talking about herself and her feelings, by gaining insight into her situation, which would in turn help her to see the way forward. The counsellor was a facilitator, asking the right questions, steering her in the right direction, taking the cues from her, so that she was in control. That was important at a time when she felt that she did not have any control. Already she was feeling that a load was being lifted from her.

As she ate the last of her sandwich and sipped the juice, she wondered why she had not gone to see someone before. Basically, the question answered itself—she knew that when you were depressed, things seemed hopeless, and you lacked the mental energy, the positive mind-set necessary to put the process of help in motion.

What a relief it was when that process started. Shay had had a lot to do with that start. Now she wondered about falling for him. Would that add to or detract from the healing process? All was positive so far, but if he did not return her feelings, where would she be then? As each day went by, she wanted him more and more to return her feelings. And, of course, she could not presume that he would, now or ever. She felt that she had to hide her feelings from him.

Maybe the last thing he wanted now was to get involved with another woman, unless on a superficial basis. She knew that he found her attractive from the way he looked at her, spoke to her. There were vibes between them that were unmistakable. No doubt he would not say no to her becoming his lover if she were to offer or indicate that she was interested. But as for something more, something more permanent, it was too soon for any of that. Not that she was about to offer herself to him. She smiled to herself at the thought. For one thing, her confidence was at a low ebb. Risking rejection was not on the agenda right now. Take it a day at a time, the counsellor had told her. The future would gradually become clearer when her mood lifted.

Back in the operating suite, meeting up with the small group again, she was able to put most of that out of her mind, which was one of the benefits of an absorbing job.

'Now, we're going to have a talk about the protocols that are part of the set-up in this particular hospital, in this particular department,' the tutor said. 'They are protocols for patient safety and staff safety to cut down on the numbers of mistakes that get made in hospitals, an attempt to think ahead instead of in retrospect.'

The afternoon went by quickly, filled with absorbing tasks and information imparted by the tutor. Deirdre felt her mind buzzing with the unfamiliar stimulation, of having to think about things that she had almost forgotten. It made her realize that her world had narrowed down, even though in her other job she had learned different and useful skills. Operating room nursing would reintroduce her to a different kind of stress, a stress that could only be controlled when you were very good at your job, well trained, well organized, up to date, when you knew what you were capable of doing and what you were not. Once she had been very good at her job—she would be again.

CHAPTER SIX

THE house was old, very beautiful, set in its own grounds, and much too big for two people, Deirdre had thought when she and the children had driven up to Shay's house on Boxing Day afternoon.

It was a sprawling building, covered with cedar shingles that had been painted a dark purple-blue colour after the local heritage fashion. It stood in a lovely garden, which looked inviting even in winter, on the edge of Prospect Bay, where both farmland and forest encroached on the dwelling places of humans, exerting the influence of nature. Or perhaps it was really the other way round, she had thought as they had driven up the circular driveway, that humans had encroached on the natural habitat of animals and birds and were themselves the aliens.

Now, with dinner over, Deirdre and Shay sat in a spacious sitting room in front of a roaring log fire. The room extended the whole depth of the house, with large windows at either end. Floodlights at back and front outside illuminated a few snowflakes falling to the ground against a backdrop of very tall fir trees, which made the inside seem very warm and protected. The room was panelled in dark golden-coloured wood and the large fireplace was built of local stone. There was a magical feeling to the whole scene. Although she knew Prospect Bay well, she had seldom been out to the more rural residential areas, although she supposed this could hardly be called rural. As far as she was concerned, she could have been in a foreign country. Shay had told her that he also owned an apartment not far from the hospital.

Deirdre and Shay were drinking coffee and she was also sipping Grand Marnier between mouthfuls of coffee. Shay had a glass of brandy on the table beside him. For the first time in a long time she was conscious of being overwhelmingly happy—it seemed to flow though her like a warm tide. Whenever she looked at him, he also seemed more relaxed and happier than she had seen him in the short time of their acquaintance. They sat opposite each other, he in a chair and she on a wide sofa.

'Dad, could you give us a hand with the computer, please?' Mark stood in the doorway and then advanced into the room. 'We're having a bit of trouble with one of the new games.' He was a tall, thin boy, very much like Shay, Deirdre thought again as she turned to look at him.

When they had first met, before dinner, he had seemed serious and shy, then he had relaxed more as Fleur and Mungo had talked to him at the dinner table. Both 'her' children, Deirdre thought, could be very sociable and charming, good conversationalists, when they wanted to be. In Mark they seemed to sense a loneliness, and they had risen to the occasion, with the result that the three of them now seemed to be on the way to becoming friends. Mark had warmed to her as well over the course of dinner, as she had striven to be as natural with him as possible, not to let her feelings for his father influence her attitude to him, not trying to impress him or make him like her. If he did like her, she would be gratified, but she wasn't going out of her way to force anything.

Shay had given Mark some new computer games for Christmas, and the three children had gone up to his room to try them out.

Shay stood up. 'Sure,' he said. 'Excuse me for about five minutes, Deirdre.'

'Yes, excuse me for taking him away from you,' Mark said to her politely. 'He's something of a computer whiz, so I expect he'll be back in a few minutes.'

'That's all right,' she said.

She took the opportunity to go to the bathroom, where she splashed cold water onto her heated face. Looking at herself in the mirror, she saw that her eyes were soft and expectant, instead of having the usual tense look of worry that stared back at her habitually from mirrors these days. Usually she tried to avoid looking at her reflection. She applied a little lip gloss and eye shadow, then brushed her hair.

As she pushed the half-open sitting-room door, it was suddenly pulled open and she almost fell against Shay, who was coming out.

'Oh…sorry,' she said, coming up close to him.

'It didn't take long,' he said. 'I thought I would get some more hot coffee…' His voice trailed off as his eyes locked with hers and she felt her lips part of their own volition in expectation. 'Would you like some?'

'I…um…' she said.

When his hand grasped her upper arm and pulled her into the room, up against his body, she did not protest. Then when he kicked the door closed, gently, she was in his arms and his mouth was on hers, demandingly, his arms around her, holding her tightly against the length of his body. With a sigh of capitulation she relaxed against him, putting up her arms to encircle his neck as a wave of heat and longing enveloped her like an electric current.

'Deirdre…' He whispered her name as he took his mouth from hers. 'I thought I would go mad if I couldn't kiss you. I'm just about out of my mind.'

Me, too, she said inwardly. 'Oh…' she said, closing her eyes and lifting her face up to him. Darling Shay, darling, darling… She wanted to say the words out loud but couldn't. Then speech was not possible as his mouth crushed hers hungrily, as though he had not kissed a woman for a very long time, and she responded like a person in a desert when they saw water. That thought came to her, so that a delirious desire to laugh welled up in her…a happiness that she had not known existed.

His hand stroked down over her hip, then up to her breast, his palm moving gently over the soft, yielding flesh, the movement bringing such pleasure to her that she felt her knees go weak, and she leaned her weight against him.

Shay pulled back from her, supporting her weight against his body. The expression of intense desire and warmth in his expression told her all that she needed to know of what he was feeling, and she did not feel surprise when he said huskily, 'I wish I could take you to bed.' He smiled down at her, so that she felt as though she were melting into him, with no vestiges of will left. I love you, she wanted to say. Instead, she stared back at him mutely, a half-smile on her face, knowing that she must look as dazed as she felt.

'That's…rather difficult right now,' she said. Having had the obvious stated, they both began to laugh, so that in a moment they were laughing helplessly.

Shay turned the large key that was in the lock of the heavy wood door to the room. 'Am I to take that,' he said, grinning down at her as he grasped her upper arms, 'as wholehearted consent, Ms Warwick?'

'I…well…' she said. 'I would rather not commit myself at

this moment. What I mean is…it is not outside the realms of possibility…but, please, do not take that as actual consent…'

She began to laugh again, moved by the comic expression on his face as he took her hand and walked with her to the very large sofa that flanked one side of the fireplace.

'I can see that you are very adept at prevarication, Ms Warwick,' he said mockingly, as he sat down and pulled her down beside him.

'Just being practical,' she answered back. 'And, please, don't tease me by calling me Ms Warwick, because I shall have to retaliate by calling you sir, and that would completely destroy the mood, which I'm rather enjoying.'

'Very well,' he said, stroking her face, holding her cheek with his hand, moving his thumb sensually over her parted lips. Then very slowly he brought his face down to hers, while he held her still in his grasp, so that she felt herself trembling inside with anticipation, her lips parting to receive him.

Gently he moved his mouth on hers as she fell against him. Then she knew that she did not have to tell him how she felt. Her body was giving her away, with every responsive move that she made. Indeed, she was a person in a desert dying of thirst, in sight of that which could save her.

Abruptly she moved back from him, jumped to her feet and looked down at him. With her back to the fireplace, they looked at each other for a long moment while she tried to get her breathing to a normal rate and to find her voice.

'I…think we're getting a little ahead of ourselves, Shay,' she said. Although she desperately wanted to be in his arms, she had the feeling that this was too soon. Besides, she felt she was somewhat out of her depth and did not know how to proceed.

'Perhaps,' he said. 'Perhaps not. I want you. I prefer to be honest.'

'Tell me that on a freezing, wet Monday morning when work is hectic, you've arrived late, been up most of the night working and you have a cold,' she said, more agitated by his words than she wanted to admit. She wanted to take him with open arms, yet something held her back. Perhaps it was that he had told her he did not trust love. 'We've had too much wine.'

He laughed. 'All right,' he said. 'That gives me plenty of opportunity...the wet Monday thing.'

Deirdre smiled back, regaining some of the sense of fun that had been with them not long before, and went to unlock the door and open it. If Fleur and Mungo came down, she did not want them to find her behind a locked door. As she returned to the fireside, Shay stood up to meet her.

'I will ask you, Deirdre,' he said quietly, taking her hands. 'I promise you that.'

'I'll deal with that when it arises,' she said with dignity, so that he laughed again.

'I shall look forward to the exchange,' he said. 'Now, how about that second cup of coffee that I was going to make?'

'Yes, please. Let me help you.'

He took her hand and led her through the house to the kitchen, where she and the children had helped earlier to prepare the dinner, which had indeed been of leftover turkey in a delicious white sauce, served with Basmati rice and an assortment of fresh vegetables. Deirdre refrained from commenting on things she saw in the house, apart from her initial remark that it was a lovely place when they had arrived.

'You could get the cups out,' he said, indicating a cupboard. 'Tell me how things are going with custody of the children.' The last remark he added casually as he filled an electric kettle with water. 'You told me that their grandmother wanted to make you guardian in the event of her death.'

'Yes,' Deirdre said, placing two cups and saucers on the

counter top. 'Anyway, I've agreed…because I don't see what else I can do.' She fumbled in a drawer for teaspoons, not sure how much more she should tell him of her private affairs, wanting to blurt it all out but wondering if he was just being polite in showing an interest. Her first instinct was that he genuinely wanted to know. Of course, she had already told him a lot.

There was a tension of awareness between them now, strong where it had been more tentative before. It was both physical and emotional. She sensed that when she looked at him her feelings would be there in her eyes.

'Of course,' she went on, 'I may never need to take that on in actuality, because Fiona's in good health, even though she's in her mid-seventies, and Mungo's almost fourteen and Fleur's twelve…I expect I told you that before.' Deirdre turned to face him, watching him spoon ground coffee into a glass coffee-maker.

'Yes, but, please, go on,' he said. 'I want to know.'

'Well, these days a child is adult at sixteen, can leave home—as you know,' she went on. 'If Mungo goes to university, that's only four more years to go…six with Fleur. Of course, in terms of my own life, it's a long time.'

Shay stopped what he was doing and turned to look at her. To her he looked overwhelmingly attractive in the loose white shirt that he was wearing, unbuttoned at the neck, and black trousers that fitted his taut figure to perfection. Having been in his arms, she was having difficulty staying back from him. Of course, she didn't have to. She had only to say the word… But there was little privacy for them.

'Yes,' he agreed. They looked at each other, attuned to the realization that she did not want to wait to have a life of her own. 'I understand that the stepfather isn't happy with that? You being the guardian?'

'No,' she said tensely, wishing he wouldn't look at her so

astutely. The colour was rising in her cheeks. 'He isn't. He's fighting it. I…I feel so sad for the children because he doesn't care about them. He pretends when he feels he has to, to keep up appearances or to impress someone. Not that the children want him to care, because they don't like him, but you would hope that their mother's husband would mean something.' There was a catch in her voice.

'Don't get yourself upset, sweetheart,' he said quietly. 'None of that was of your making, so don't feel you have to take that on. It's not like my situation, where I think I brought a lot of it on myself.'

That was the first time he had called her sweetheart, or used any sort of endearment, and for some reason it brought a lump to her throat. 'Another thing,' she said, unthinkingly, 'Fiona's lawyer said my chances were less because I wasn't married, and Jerry could get married and strengthen his case that way. I know he has someone, but he pretends he hasn't. When it's to his advantage, she'll come out into the open, I suspect.'

Flushed and far from calm, she became aware that she was talking too much. Shay stood and looked at her intently, con-sideringly, while the kettle emitted a shrill whistle, unheeded.

'Jerry's lawyer accused me of wanting custody of the chil-dren so that I could get some of their money,' she went on hotly, clenching her fists. 'That's not true. Until very recently, I had no idea at all that they had been left so much money. It…it's all so awful.'

'I shouldn't have brought it up, love,' he said, coming over to her. As he stood looking down at her, not doing anything, the tension built up so that she felt she would scream at him.

'Are you…are you going to kiss me, or what?' she said challengingly, 'Because I can't stand this tension. It seems to exude from you.'

Shay gave her a slow, sensual smile that made her heart do strange things. 'At least half of it is coming from you,' he said.

'Shall I…um…? Shall I pour the…um…?' She made a motion, indicating the boiling kettle.

'No, I'll do it when I'm ready,' he said. 'And, yes, I am going to kiss you, but first of all I want to ask you a question. Sorry it's not a wet Monday, but I can't wait. Will you be my lover…my mistress?'

Before she could utter a sound, he kissed her, a slow, sensual kiss that left her without resistance.

'I'll consider it,' she said weakly.

'Let me know before you leave here tonight,' he said, holding her at arm's length. The kitchen was gradually filling up with steam.

'What if I don't?' she challenged.

'I'll turn into a toad and neither of us will have another chance.'

Deirdre stared back at him, her pupils widening. His words had sent a strange chill through her, because she had been thinking a lot just lately about never having another chance at so many things. In her short life she had discovered that very often opportunities did not wait.

'Hey,' he said softly, grasping her arms and giving her a little shake, tuning in instantly to her mood. 'I can wait…'

'But you don't believe in love.'

'I said I don't trust it,' he said, still holding her by the arms, still looking down at her. 'Not that I don't, necessarily, believe in it.'

'You're…you're splitting hairs,' she said.

'Maybe.'

'We'd better make the coffee,' she said. 'If the kids come in, they'll think we're having a steam bath.'

She deliberately pulled away from him, putting some distance between them, shattered by his request and the inherent contradiction that he wanted to know soon, yet he could wait. Put subtly or baldly, it was the same. He wanted her. She wanted him. Yet she wanted him to love her, if only because she felt she was falling in love with him. Instinctively, she wanted to accept him on any terms—perhaps she was being juvenile to expect him to love her. 'Better to have loved and lost than never to have loved at all.' She could not remember who had said that, but it was part of her family lore of literature and poetry, deeply ingrained in her psyche.

At last Shay made the coffee, while she looked on restlessly. Happy in his company, she still wanted to commit herself in some way, but was not sure what to say.

'Dad!' Mark came silently into the kitchen. 'Could we have some hot chocolate, please? The three of us? I could make it.'

'I'll make it,' Shay offered, 'and we'll bring it up to you. How are the computer games going?'

'Just great,' Mark said enthusiastically.

Deirdre and Shay drank their coffee in the kitchen, while he made three mugs of hot chocolate and Deirdre got a tray ready. 'Could I take it upstairs?' she said. 'I'd like to see what they're doing.'

'Sure,' he said.

Mark had a sitting room-cum-study next to his bedroom, Shay informed her, where he did his schoolwork. He had a computer and his own television and audio equipment, so that he could have privacy if he wanted it.

'Mark seems like a very nice boy,' she had remarked to Shay when his son had gone upstairs again.

'He is, most of the time,' Shay had agreed. 'He's had a lot of material things, but a bit of a rough deal when it comes to parental attention. I've tried hard, but the reality of my job is that I have to be away from him a fair amount. Since Tony—Antonia—left, I've cut back on my work hours as much as possible but, as you know, when you're a surgeon you have to be available for emergencies and post-op care, elective cases, and so on. It's a labour-intensive job. There's a fine balance between delegating and being responsible oneself.'

'I understand,' she had said. The mention of his wife left her with an unfamiliar feeling of jealousy, an emotion that she despised and which she seldom felt. In spite of his denial, perhaps he still cared for Antonia, and would have her back instantly if she were to offer.

The prospect of it left her with a curious feeling of bleakness. Knowing him had shown her a glimpse of a life that had, up to the time of their meeting, not seemed a reality for her, a life in which she was attracted to an intelligent, kind, devastatingly attractive professional man who wanted her—sexually, if not in any other way. Just thinking about him when they were not together left her in a state of pleasurably agitated awe. Yet he was really the most down-to-earth man, easy to talk to, who actually listened with all his attention. That was a quality in itself that was very attractive, beyond measure. Very few people were good listeners, she had discovered. In order to be a good listener, you had to care about other people, not be focused on yourself all the time.

'It's a pity he's an only child. Maybe if he had siblings he wouldn't be so lonely, although I know that relationships between siblings are not all sweetness and light.' He turned to grin at her as he made the drinks with hot milk. 'On the positive side, he has good friends…apart from those he got into trouble with. They've stuck with him through bad times.'

As Deirdre climbed the stairs, carefully carrying the tray holding three mugs of hot chocolate, her thoughts and emotions were churning as she thought over what Shay had said about wanting her. It appeared that she could become his lover immediately, if she wanted to. No doubt he would invite her to his apartment in the city, where they could be alone, when the children were otherwise supervised. The very thought of going there to meet him, or being taken there in his car, filled her with nervousness and longing. Was it the right thing for her? They had known each other for such a short time. And did wanting something so much make it right for you?

What she had learnt in life was that you could not go on second-guessing yourself. At some point you had to make a decision and, having made it, take the plunge. If it turned out to be wrong for you, you had to acknowledge that and cut your losses, telling yourself that the decision had been right for you at the time you had made it, with the knowledge that you had had at your disposal.

All her instincts seemed to cry out that it was right for her. She let out a sigh as she reached the top of the stairs.

She heard the kids chattering and laughing, so just had to follow the sound. They seemed to be getting on like the proverbial house on fire, and she smiled to herself. 'Here's your hot chocolate,' she called.

Mark came out of his bedroom and she could see the other two in the room behind him, looking through some CDs. 'We'll have it in my computer room, please,' Mark said, indicating the room next to the bedroom, so she took the tray in there.

'Thank you, Deirdre,' he added, taking the tray from her and putting it on a side table. 'You really don't mind if I call you Deirdre…Deirdre?'

They grinned at each other and she was touched to see that he blushed. He was really more vulnerable and shy than he let on. 'Oh, no,' she said. 'Unless you want to call me Dee, like Mungo and Fleur do.'

'I'll see,' he said, considering the option. 'I really like the name Deirdre.' Then he blurted out, 'I think it's really great what you're doing with those kids…looking after them for such a long time and all that when you're so young yourself. They've told me all about it, and it's really great. My dad told me about you, too. I mean, they're not your own kids…' His voice died away, his face redder.

Quickly Deirdre moved to put him at his ease. 'Well,' she said, 'they really needed me and we liked each other from the beginning. Now I think we love each other. So it's not really like a job, more a labour of love, so to speak.' She had to be careful what she said in case he was comparing her to his own mother, so that she did not seem to imply to Mark that his mother did not love him, otherwise she would not have taken off. For one thing, she certainly did not know all the details of their family situation.

'I wish I had someone like you,' he said. The wistful note in his voice moved her so much that her throat constricted with emotion.

'Maybe we can be friends,' she said. 'After all, I'm working with your dad three days a week, so our families can certainly get together, if you would like to.'

'I would like to,' he said.

Behind Mark, on a shelf attached to the wall, Deirdre could see a framed photograph of a smiling woman, who she assumed immediately must be Mark's mother. The woman was beautiful, her skin glowing, her pale blonde hair pulled back away from her face. With her brilliant smile, slightly tanned skin, large, expressive eyes and arched eyebrows, she looked like a movie star.

'That's my mother,' Mark said matter-of-factly, following her gaze. 'Did my dad tell you about her?'

'He told me something,' she said carefully.

'She's out of the country,' he said.

'You must miss her, especially at Christmastime.'

'Yes, I do,' he said pensively. 'But I'm coming round to the idea that she has to have her own life. I just wish she was closer, that's all…in Prospect Bay, or maybe Vancouver…so that I could see her.'

'Have you told her that?' Deirdre asked gently, thinking of her own parents and how much she missed them and wished they were home. 'I expect she misses you.'

'No, I haven't told her,' he said. 'She's with a man.'

'That's all right,' Deirdre said. 'You would just be telling the truth, and very often people appreciate the truth, much more than we all think. We spend a lot of psychological energy telling people that everything's all right when it isn't.'

'Do you think she would come back if I said that?' he asked. 'I don't mean come back to my dad. I think that's all over—they don't even like each other any more. I mean, would she come back for me?'

'I think she very well might,' Deirdre said, a mixture of emotions making her voice tremble a little as she recognized twinges of jealousy in herself at the image of the beautiful Antonia and the prospect of her being back. 'You'll never know if you don't ask.'

Feeling that she was maybe shooting herself in the foot, Deirdre nevertheless persisted in giving this rather lost boy some gentle advice. Not that she really thought she herself had much of a chance with Shay, of being anything to him permanently. She just knew that at the moment he did not have a woman in his life and that he appeared to like her. Perhaps it would not matter to her whether his ex-wife were here or not, in terms of any possibilities with him, other than the purely physical ones. Then she recalled how Shay's eyes lit up when he looked at her, with desire, hungry for her. At those times the tension was almost unbearable because the feeling was reciprocated, yet she was loath to make it obvious. She hoped that her eyes did not blaze at him in the way his did when he looked at her. A lack of reciprocation of her love on his part was something that gave her an odd sense of mourning.

Of course, she had been aware that at first Shay had tried to hide his lust for her, or whatever it was, but as time had gone by he had given way to it.

She could not tell Mark that she was in love with his father, yet maybe she didn't have to. He was an intelligent and astute boy who would obviously be wondering about her relationship with his father, putting two and two together and coming up with four. The more he saw of the two of them together, the more obvious it would become.

'What about…him?' Mark said hesitantly. 'The man?'

'That's something about which she will have to decide,' Deirdre said. 'You don't have to do anything about him, or worry about him. After all, you were part of your mother's life long before he appeared on the scene. You have a right to have your say.' Then she laughed deprecatingly. 'It's easy to give someone else advice, isn't it, Mark? That's what I'm doing. It's not so easy to get one's own life in order. I think it helps to listen to advice and comment, even if you don't follow it. It's nice that someone else should take the time to think about what's happening to you. I go to a counsellor myself, and just hearing myself talk is a great eye-opener. I think afterwards, Did I really think that, or feel that? You gain insight, which is what really changes things…if you let it.'

'I'm having counselling too,' he said. 'Why…why are you having counselling—if you don't mind me asking?' His blush deepened, and Deirdre had the urge, which she resisted, to give him a hug. Maybe that would come later, when and if she got to know him better.

'Well...' she began, wondering how she could put it, 'I was under a lot of stress because I wanted to go back to work as a nurse, and didn't see how I could do it. I suppose you could say that I had...have...too many responsibilities and not enough time for myself. Something like that. And my parents and brother are out of the country, so I feel alone sometimes. It's not easy to explain.'

'I know what you mean,' he said, very seriously.

'I just knew that something was wrong,' she said, 'and I didn't know what to do about it. I knew I needed help.'

'I know that feeling,' he said quietly, sadly.

'Hey, Dee!' Fleur came into the room, her face flushed and excited. 'We don't have to go yet, do we? We're having so much fun.'

'Not just yet,' she said, 'but I don't want to leave it too late, as I have to drive us home and the old car might give me trouble if there's snow on the road. I'll call up to you when it's time to go. Here's some hot chocolate for you.'

'OK. Thanks.'

'See you later, Mark,' she said, smiling at him.

As she went down the stairs, Deirdre smiled to herself at the irony of giving advice to someone else when she herself found her own life more than she could comfortably cope with at the moment.

An hour later, when she and Shay had spent an enjoyable time talking to each other in front of the fire in the sitting room about everything that occurred to them, laughing a lot, it was time to depart. They had managed to skirt around anything really very personal. Many times Deirdre had had to remind herself of the brief time that she had known Shay, yet it seemed that somehow the idea of him had always been in her consciousness, as though in shadow, just out of reach, all her life. It was a very odd feeling and, contemplating it, she wondered if she were going mad. She understood that love, attraction could do strange things to you. It was almost a sense of precognition.

She could see through the windows that a light snow was still falling, although not settling much on the ground, not enough to make the roads particularly dangerous.

'Have you snow tyres on your car?' Shay asked her as he helped her into her coat in the front hall. The children were just outside the front door, their outer gear on, throwing snowballs at each other with the meagre amount of snow that they could collect from shrubs and grass.

'Yes,' she said.

'When you're going down the hill,' he said, 'it's better to stay in first gear, right down to the flat ground, because the road here can be very slippery, even if it doesn't look it. There's black ice sometimes, so you take care.'

Touched by his concern, Deirdre smiled up at him. 'I'll keep that advice in mind,' she said. 'Thank you so much, Shay, for a great dinner and a lovely evening. I haven't enjoyed myself so much for a very long time. I…I'll see you at work.'

'Thank you for coming,' he said. 'It's been delightful for me and for Mark.' He bent forward and kissed her, moving his lips warmly and gently over hers, putting a hand up to stroke her hair in a gesture that was totally intimate and loving. 'If you're wondering, this is not the home I had with Antonia. That was sold. Neither Mark nor I were particularly attached to it, and we didn't want to stay there with all the memories, some of which were not good. Mark and I chose this house—we fell in love with it, you might say.'

'It feels like a home, not just a house, and it's beautiful,' she said, glad that he had told her, as she had indeed been wondering. She returned his kiss gently, not touching him otherwise, closing her eyes, aware of the children through the slightly open doorway that let in a blast of cold air.

'If you have an answer for me,' he murmured, holding her gaze intently so that she could not look away, 'please, put me out of my suspense. If you can take me as you find me, we may be all right together. I prefer to be up-front and honest, and I would be lying if I said I could offer you any kind of future. But I find you totally captivating. I'm not sure why, I can't put it into words right now—and I can't imagine what you see in a cynic like me, although I know that you do see something.'

With burning cheeks, wishing she could deal with this in a cool, sophisticated way, Deirdre moistened her dry lips with her tongue. Her emotions were moving her this way and that, so that she felt like an animal in a cage, pacing up and down. Yet it was a confinement that she wanted because it would be with the man she loved. Yes, she had to admit it fully now. It thrilled and frightened her at the same time, and she knew she could not tell him of her love, not yet, because it left her totally vulnerable and she was not sure that she wanted him to know that now.

'I…I'm not a very sophisticated person when it comes to being propositioned by a man,' she said, trying to make light of it, when her heart was pounding with an unfamiliar excitement and a fear that she might blow it. 'It's not something that happens every day.'

When he grinned down at her, she felt herself going weak at the knees again. 'I like you just the way you are,' he said. 'I don't want a hard, calculating, cynical woman.'

'But you're a cynic,' she said. 'You said it yourself.'

'Two cynics don't go well together, I think,' he said. 'I have a strong suspicion that you could soften me, Deirdre, if you wanted to.'

The attraction between them was so strong that she knew she could not refuse…it was unthinkable. Yet it was so much more than a pure physical attraction for her. Very slowly she drew on her thin leather driving gloves over hands that were trembling, stalling for time.

She took in a deep, tremulous breath and let it out on a sigh. Her throat felt tight with emotion, so that she was not sure she could even speak. Glad of the dim, soft light in the hall, so that her hectic colour was not so apparent, she cleared her throat. 'The answer's yes,' she said, feeling her cheeks flush an even darker colour and hearing her own voice high-pitched with nervousness. 'But…not yet. I need to get used to the idea. You understand?'

'Yes.' He whispered the word, as his eyes seemed to burn into hers and he caressed her cheek with his warm hand. 'Darling…sweetheart.'

'Did you…did you call your wife that?' The words came out as of their own volition. 'I think I'm jealous of her.'

'No, I didn't call her either of those words. I called her "honey", mostly, a word that has long since lost its appeal,' he said softly. 'All that is over. I'm a different person now. Things were dead between us long before we decided to part. We kept up a home for Mark. You don't have to be jealous, believe me, although I'm flattered. You're a very lovely woman, Deirdre, in all respects. You don't have any idea, do you?'

She shook her head. 'You can tell me as often as you like,' she said.

'I'll wait for you,' he said. Then he kissed her again, while the kids shouted and laughed outside, as though they thought it was perfectly all right for the older generation to be taking such a long time to say goodnight, if they thought about it at all.

'I…don't know whether being your lover adds to my dilemmas or detracts from them,' she said, daring to utter her thoughts, with a deprecating laugh.

'We'll work to make it the latter, shall we?' he said, his mouth quirking in the slight smile that she found so attractive, his eyes warm.

'You want to be honest, Shay. So do I. Will it make my life more complex?'

'I expect it will. In a good way, I hope,' he said. 'I want to be good to you and good for you, Deirdre. If you want to talk, I'll be there to listen.'

'Thank you,' she said.

'I never cease to marvel and be glad that you literally crossed my path,' he said.

As she, Mungo and Fleur got into her car, after Shay had brushed off the snow from all windows with a garden broom, Mark said, 'Be careful going down the mountain. It's what the newscasters call treacherous.'

'This is not exactly a mountain,' Mungo said, having wound down his window about six inches.

'I know,' Mark said, 'but it sounds better than calling it a big hill, and, as you know, the road winds round and round, like on a mountain.'

At that remark, Mungo began to sing—or rather, bawl— the old song, 'She'll be Coming Round the Mountain When She Comes'. The other two kids joined in.

'She'll be riding on a float plane when she comes…' Mark yelled unmusically. Deirdre and Shay grinned at each other as she sat in the driver's seat, and he stood near her, hunched up in a light jacket that he had thrown on hastily against the cold.

'That's the result of expensive music lessons,' he said to her, bending down to her level and the partially open car window.

'Not quite the end result, I hope. Anyway, that's life,' she said. 'And you can lead a horse to water, but you can't make it drink. There are two clichés for you that are very useful when raising children, so I've found.'

'Indeed,' he said, his breath coming out in small white clouds. 'You take care, now. Remember what I said about first gear and black ice.'

'I will. Goodnight.'

'Goodnight. Come on, Mark. Time to go in.'

The raucous song came to an end as she turned on the engine and put the car into first gear.

As she steered her old car away from the house, Deirdre revelled in an exhilarating mood of happiness. Could she trust it? For now, she wasn't going to think about that. Sufficient unto the day…

'I really enjoyed being there,' Fleur said. 'It was great. I like Mark a lot.'

'Yeah, it was really great,' Mungo agreed.

Deirdre smiled.

CHAPTER SEVEN

A WEEK after the new year, Deirdre received a telephone call early in the morning from the head nurse of the operating suite. It was a Monday.

'Deirdre,' she said, 'I'm calling to see if you could work the night shift tonight instead of the day shift. I hate to ask you, seeing that you've been here for such a short time and the nights can be hectic, but I've had two of the night nurses call in sick with this flu that's going around. You haven't got any symptoms yourself, I hope?'

'No…no, I haven't,' Deirdre managed to say, feeling dazed. She had been up for about ten minutes and was rushing around, getting ready to go to the hospital.

'There will be two other nurses on the night shift with you,' the head nurse went on. 'We often get emergencies, some trauma. A lot of the more serious trauma goes to University Hospital, as you know. When the nurses called in sick, I thought of you because you've had trauma experience at University Hospital. I don't know how I'm going to staff this place. A lot of the day nurses have called in sick as well.'

'I…well…I could do the night shift,' Deirdre said, mindful of the short time that she had been in the department, 'if you think I could cope with it.'

'The other two RNs are old hands,' the head nurse went on, 'so you would have to scrub for cases, while they do the organizing and circulating. You'll be all right doing that. I may have to ask you to do that shift until the others are back.'

'All right,' Deirdre agreed, her mind working quickly to organize in a few seconds how she would juggle where Mungo and Fleur would sleep and how their grandmother would cope with looking after them. After all, they could cook and do a lot for themselves, and their grandmother as well. She didn't want to put everything onto Fiona when she herself was being paid to look after them. It would be a compromise between them, she decided then and there.

'If you're wondering why I'm here so early,' the head nurse went on grimly, 'I thought I would get here to try to organize my skeleton staff. If this epidemic gets much worse, we'll have to shut down the department to elective cases. Thank you very much, Deirdre. We'll see you at about eleven-fifteen tonight. God willing, I don't expect be here myself, but you never can tell.'

Deirdre put down the receiver. She was in her parents' home and the whistling kettle she had plugged in for coffee was shrilling. What now? She could go back to bed and try to sleep some more, or she could carry on and have breakfast, then try to sleep a bit in the afternoon in preparation for having to be up all night. Right now she felt wide awake and didn't think she could sleep, having psyched herself up to go to work.

After dithering for a few seconds she decided to make the coffee and get something to eat. There were things she could do at home. Later on she would telephone Fiona and tell her of the change of plan. Mungo and Fleur were at Fiona's house. What she could do was drive over there and take them to school. They seemed to be adapting well to her schedule of work and rather liked having three homes. Deirdre herself would check Jerry's house to make sure all was well there, as he was still away. She was glad that she was not being paid by him.

The cat brushed against her legs as she sat at the kitchen table, drinking her coffee, contemplating what she might have to cope with during the night shift. As well as dealing with any emergencies that came in, the nurses had to prepare the operating rooms for the elective cases the next day, which was a very time-consuming job.

The one regret that she had about not working the day shift was that she would not be seeing Shay. Then it dawned on her that he would be one of the senior surgeons on call at night for emergencies, as Monday was his operating day. If there was anything that the senior surgical resident could not deal with, he would be there. With that in mind, she decided that she didn't mind at all.

Quickly she finished her breakfast, got dressed and then put a call through to Fiona.

The kids hugged her when she walked into Fiona's kitchen. 'Dee!' Fleur exclaimed when she saw her. 'I'm missing you. Are you driving us to school? When are we going to get together with Mark again?'

'One question at a time, please.' Deirdre laughed. 'Yes, I'm driving you. As for seeing Mark, we have to pick a good day then see if it's good for him, too, and invite him for supper, or whatever.'

'Let's do it soon, Mungo said.

Much later, Deirdre was in the OR nurses' locker room at the Stanton Memorial Hospital. It was ten minutes to eleven that evening and she had already changed into a pale blue two-piece scrub suit when the two other nurses burst into the room. They were both in early middle age, looked tough and what the head nurse had called old hands. She had not met either of them before.

'Hi!' one said cheerfully to her. 'You must be Deirdre. Good of you to come in at such short notice. The other two who usually work with us are in bed coughing their guts out right now.' She chuckled. 'I'm Myra and this is Marge.'

The other nurse shook hands with Deirdre. 'Pleased to meet you,' she said. 'People usually call us the two Ms, because we usually get to work together on night duty. You stick close to us, kid, and you'll be all right. What we haven't seen and done in this game isn't worth knowing.'

Deirdre laughed. 'I'll do that,' she said. 'Very pleased to meet you.'

As the two other nurses quickly changed from their outdoor gear into scrub suits and white slip-on clogs, they kept up a running commentary about what she should expect.

'When we get in there,' Myra said, 'the first thing we do is check the drugs with the senior nurse on the evening shift, then she gives us the drug keys. Our routine work is that we have to restock all the operating rooms, then we check the operating list for tomorrow and get each room ready for all the elective cases.'

'We get on with the restocking right away, we don't hang about, and we work as quickly as we possibly can, because if we get emergencies, the routine work gets put aside,' Marge added. 'You and I will get on with that. Myra's in charge, so the first thing she will do is make sure that two rooms are absolutely ready for emergencies—one is a general surgery room and the other is a gynae room, as we get a lot of obstetrics and gynaecological emergency cases here.'

'I see.' Deirdre nodded, glad that she had these two nurses to work with on her first night.

'Since we usually have four nurses on nights,' Myra said, 'we've got our work cut out for us. The trick is to be absolutely ready for anything first of all, then work like hell to get the routine stuff done. You just watch what we do.'

'OK.'

'And I forgot to say, if there are cases going on from the evening shift, we have to take over there before we can get on with our own work. When we come on, we pray that there won't be any ongoing cases. If there are, two of us usually deal with those, while the others get on with the routine work, if we can. Sometimes all four of us just have to deal with the ongoing cases.'

When they got into the main part of the operating suite they were relieved to find the senior nurse on the evening shift sitting in the small office that was occupied by the head nurse during the day. 'All quiet,' she said cheerfully, before they could ask the question.

'Thank God for that,' Myra said. 'I feel like having a bit of respite tonight.'

'Amen to that,' Marge said.

'But it's an eerie silence,' the evening nurse said ruminatively, 'I can feel in my bones that something will happen.'

'Oh, shut up!' Marge said. 'You're going to jinx us, or something.'

'She's usually right,' Myra said, giving Deirdre a conspiratorial wink. 'She's got psychic powers.'

'You're freaking me out,' Marge said. 'Come on, let's check those drugs.'

'You phone Emergency, Marge,' Myra said, 'to see what they've got in there that could come our way. I'll show Deirdre how we check the drugs.'

'Okey-dokey,' Marge said.

Deirdre followed Myra and the evening nurse, feeling as

though she wanted to roar with laughter, again realizing how lucky she was to have landed up with these two. She could have found herself with a couple of irritable, unhelpful individuals. These two women had missed their vocation, she thought. They should have been stand-up comics. On second thoughts, they must be two of the best nurses in the whole operating suite, she estimated shrewdly, having met many. Probably two of the best in the whole hospital. If she could evolve to be like them, she would be contented with herself professionally.

'Did you get any sleep today, Deirdre?' Myra asked.

'Not a wink,' Deirdre admitted. 'I tried, but just couldn't sleep. I'm feeling a bit punch-drunk right now.'

'Don't you worry,' Myra said, as the evening-shift nurse unlocked the drug cupboard, which was in a prominent position in the main OR corridor. 'In no time at all you'll have so much adrenaline surging through your body that you'll feel that sleep will elude you for the rest of your life.'

'I'm looking forward to it,' she said.

'The anaesthetist on call tonight is Dr Burns…good old Chuck,' the evening nurse informed them.

'Oh, super!' Myra said. 'He's such a darling. You've met him, Deirdre?'

'Yes. And I agree with you that he's a darling.'

'And the general surgeons are Shay Melburne and Boris Barovsky, plus the usual auxiliary bods.'

'Right you are,' Myra said nonchalantly, while Deirdre's heart quickened at the sound of Shay's name. She had mixed feelings about seeing him, because it could mean that they would be working non-stop all night, with no time for even a cup of tea or coffee.

'This cupboard here,' Myra informed Deirdre, pointing to a glass-fronted cupboard next to the main drug cupboard, 'houses the sterile emergency tracheostomy set. Everything you could possibly want for a tracheostomy is there, including the local anaesthetic drugs. This here…' she indicated a compact box with a handle '…is what we call the stab tracheostomy set. When you get a patient in with a blocked airway, turning blue—usually a kid with acute epiglottitis—and you don't want to mess about trying to do a cut-down tracheostomy with a scalpel, you stab the trocar here into the trachea. Of course, not many people can do that with any accuracy—it's best to get an ENT surgeon. Some anaesthetists are pretty good at it. This saves the lives of a lot of kids.'

Deirdre nodded. 'I'll remember,' she said.

As it turned out, Deirdre was not to be disappointed in the two nurses. Her respect for them rose as time went by. A nurse like either of them could save the professional life of many a quaking, dithering junior doctor who came within their orbit. They knew what to do for anything and everything that came in.

At a near running pace, she and Marge began to stock the rooms, putting out everything from latex surgical gloves to plastic endotracheal tubes to replenish stock used during the day.

It was at two o'clock in the morning when the telephone shrilled, causing the three nurses to emerge from various rooms into the corridor like rabbits out of a warren, while Myra headed for the nearest inter-departmental phone.

'Hello? OR here,' she said in a loud voice, while the other two waited for the news. 'Yep…Yep…Yep. We can be ready in five minutes. Give me the name of the patient, Shay. And he's still in Emergency? Right… Right. Do you want me to contact Chuck Burns, or will you do it? Oh, good…thanks. See you shortly.'

'What's up?' Marge said to Myra, as she stood by the door of a room from which she had emerged.

'Ruptured appendix for Shay,' Myra said. 'We'll do it in room one. He's going to do a standard laparotomy incision, seeing as the thing is ruptured. He's going to contact Chuck. One less thing for us to do, and the senior surgical resident is in Emergency already, and the intern is coming up. Would you like to scrub, Deirdre?'

It wasn't really a question, more like an order. 'Er...yes,' Deirdre said, knowing that she could cope quite well with a standard laparotomy, a central incision into the abdominal cavity. Often, if the appendix had not ruptured, they would make an appendix incision, just a small incision in the right lower part of the abdomen, called McBurney's point. But since it had ruptured, and the contents of the gut would be leaking out into the abdominal cavity, they needed a much bigger incision in order to have a good look around inside and suction out all the material that had leaked out. In the old days, and sometimes in modern times, peritonitis could result from a ruptured appendix. Death had often resulted in the days before antibiotics. It was something that had to be dealt with immediately.

All this went through Deirdre's mind as she and Marge went to room one, which was set up for general surgical emergencies.

'You get scrubbed, Deirdre,' Marge said, 'while I open up the packs. What size gloves do you take?'

'Six and a half, please,' she said, pausing at the scrub sinks, which were just outside the door of room one, to put on a disposable surgical mask over her nose and mouth, to tuck stray hair under the paper cap that she wore and to put on a pair of plastic goggles that she kept in her pocket. Quickly she started the scrub procedure, taking a sterile nailbrush, lathering her hands with liquid soap from a special container that was operated by a foot pedal, opening the taps, which had levers on them so that they could be turned off with the elbows at the end of the scrub procedure.

In the operating room she put on a sterile gown, while Marge tied up the back of it, then she put on her gloves. Marge had opened up packs of drapes and instruments for a major abdominal operation, as well as large gauze sponges and sutures.

A calm descended on Deirdre as she surveyed the equipment in front of her, aware that she knew exactly what to do, step by step. She would prepare her set-up in the order in which the surgeon would need to use the instruments and equipment. In that way, the scrub nurse was always ready, always at least one step ahead of the surgeon, even if she had only minutes to scrub before he scrubbed himself. First, they had to prep the skin of the patient with a disinfectant iodine solution…

Quickly she collected her thoughts and went to work, the adrenaline running through her bloodstream, as Myra had predicted it would. That, she hoped, would compensate for her tiredness, for not having slept that day. She felt that sense of rather sick excitement that she always felt before an operation as she geared herself up mentally to meet the challenge. She gave a passing thought to Mungo and Fleur, sleeping peacefully, she hoped, in their granny's house.

Myra had arranged for a porter to transport the patient, a young man, on a stretcher from the emergency department. Deirdre heard when they arrived outside the room. Moments later the senior surgical resident, Dr Ross Chandler, and the surgical intern, Dr Eleanor Chan, came into the room. They looked tired, with that drawn, pale look of the chronically overworked. Deirdre felt for them.

'Howdy, all,' Ross Chandler said laconically, his voice matching his tall, thin body. 'Nice to see you all again.'

'And we just love to see you, too. How sure are you about this diagnosis, Ross?' Myra asked the resident. 'I want to get some idea of how long we're likely to be here.'

'Pretty sure,' he said. 'Shay agrees.'

'That's enough for me.'

The double doors to the room were pushed open and the anaesthetist, Dr Chuck Burns, came into the room, pushing the patient ahead of him on the stretcher.

The young man on the stretcher looked pale and sick and scared. Myra moved into high gear, talking to him to ease his fears, explaining all that would happen to him, helping him shift over onto the operating table, while Dr Burns filled in during the pauses, telling him what he proposed to do next.

Deirdre glanced quickly at them, then away again, getting on with the task of setting up her instruments, tearing open packets of surgical catgut. Marge had given her a card that listed all the sutures that she would need to prepare for Shay and Marge had stuck the card up on the wall with sticky tape.

To say that Deirdre felt nervous was putting it mildly. It had been quite a while since she had scrubbed for such a case, but it was something that one did not forget. More to the point, she wondered what Shay would think when he saw her there, a nurse barely out of orientation.

Then suddenly there he was, coming into the room, tying on his surgical mask.

'Good morning, everyone,' he said quietly, going over to the side of the operating table to talk to the patient. It did not take long for the anaesthetist to have the patient under the influence of an anaesthetic, at which point Shay turned his attention to her, to see who he had as a scrub nurse.

'Deirdre! Is it you?' he looked at her closely. 'What are you doing here in the middle of the night?'

'Um…the flu epidemic,' she said, feeling suddenly tongue-tied. 'I…was asked to fill in.'

Their eyes met and they smiled at each other, the interaction not particularly noticed by the others in the room in the midst of all the activity in getting the patient positioned on the operating table. 'Ah, yes, the flu,' he said. 'I've been doing all I can to avoid getting it, but there's no sure-fire way. Anyway, it's great to see you.'

'Thank you,' she said.

'Are you ready for me?' he asked. 'I'm going to scrub now.'

'Yes, I'm ready,' she said.

'I'm going to need a corrugated rubber drain at the end,' he said, 'as there's going to be fluid to drain out to prevent abscesses forming in the abdominal cavity. And I'll probably need a Haemovac drain as well. You know all about that, don't you, Deirdre?'

'Yes,' she said, 'but thanks for reminding me.'

Before too long the skin had been prepped, the patient covered with sterile drapes, the tables and trays of instruments and sponges in place. She stood on the opposite side of the operating table from Shay. He smiled at her over the top of his surgical mask. 'Scalpel, please,' he said.

As the operation got under way, Deirdre had a sense of dissonance for a few moments. How odd it was that she should be here, doing this job, with this man, so soon after she had not been able to get off a bus, had been so low in spirits that she had not known what to do with herself, had looked at the hospital notice board to see jobs available. It seemed amazing that it had all happened, that here she was in the middle of the night, working with a man she had fallen in love with. She was by no means in control of her life, yet somehow the work had lifted her out of despair. Here she was doing something for which she was trained, something she was good at.

* * *

Somehow she got through the night. All at once, it seemed, the morning had arrived and it was time to go off duty. Somehow the three of them had got through the necessary routine work and the emergency operations as well. Awash with tiredness, she was happy when Myra and Marge let her go off duty a little ahead of time, before the day staff came on. In the deserted coffee-lounge she made herself a cup of tea, going automatically through the motions of dipping a tea-bag in a mug of boiled water.

She sipped the hot liquid standing up, fearful that if she sat down she would fall asleep. It had been a long time since a cup of tea had tasted so good. There were a few moments of quiet before the day staff came *en masse* through the door to get their morning coffee.

There was no sense of surprise in her when the door opened and Shay came in, only a sense of inevitability. 'I've been looking for you,' he said simply. 'Will you have breakfast with me at my apartment? I'm going to take the morning off, get some sleep. Please, come.' He looked as exhausted as she knew she must look.

'All right, I will come,' she said softly. 'I would like to have a shower. I'm so exhausted, I ache all over.'

'You can have a shower at my place, if you would like to,' he offered.

'All right. Thank you.'

'Finish your tea, then,' he said. 'I'll meet you in the main lobby in about ten minutes, then you can follow me in your car. It's not far.'

Deirdre nodded, as her voice seemed to have deserted her. After all, it had not been difficult, she mused as he went out as silently as he had come in. It had been almost matter-of-fact, his face serious, no banter, no embarrassment, nothing coy about it. In a way, she was glad of that. She was about to become his lover, he was ready for her and she for him. They were both tired, each wanting the comfort of the other. Perhaps it was good that they were both exhausted; that was maybe more sobering and serious than a wet Monday morning would have been, she thought.

Slowly and deliberately she changed into her outdoor clothes in the locker room, brushed her hair, picked up her bag and left. Outside the main lobby she put through a call to Fiona to make sure that all was well there, to find that they were all up, having breakfast.

Shay appeared then, and she went up to him so that he could take her arm. 'Show me where you're parked,' he said.

Moments later she was following him out of the parking lot in her car. The small apartment block where he lived when he needed to be in the centre of the town, exclusive and charming, was in a quiet residential area, no more than a mile away from the hospital. It was a small ivy-covered building of red brick, surrounded by gardens that were now covered in light snow.

'I'm on the ground floor,' Shay said to her as they emerged from their cars in the covered parking area. 'What do you like for breakfast?'

'Oh…just a glass of orange juice would be lovely,' she said. 'I'm not hungry—just very thirsty.' As she walked side by side with him it all felt so right to her, yet strange at the same time, as though it were somehow predestined and her free will had been taken away from her. She felt an odd equanimity, which surprised her. Even so, she found that she could not look at him.

A heavy-looking oak door at the entrance led into a wide hallway, then another private door led into a smaller quiet corridor, where his apartment door was the only one. Inside the apartment, all external sound was cut off—traffic noise, the sound of the wind in the trees—and they were in a quiet world of their own.

'Let me take your coat,' Shay said, his hands on her shoulders, and she let him help her shrug out of her heavy wool coat, sensitized acutely to his touch. Then she divested herself of her hat, scarf and gloves in the quiet dimness of his hallway, which smelt of lemon furniture polish and fresh flowers.

His touch on her was almost unbearable and she shivered. The need to go into his arms was one that she could not put off much longer, and she turned to him, waiting.

'Would you like your orange juice now?' he asked softly, taking off his own coat and flinging it on a chair in the hallway. 'Or would you like a shower first?'

Deirdre detected a certain humility in him, a sense that he did not take her for granted, and the love she felt for him threatened to overwhelm her. 'I…' she said. Then she went into his arms, putting her arms up around his neck, touching his neck, pulling his head down to her. 'Shay…kiss me.'

With a groan of longing he pulled her hard against him and crushed her mouth with his, while she held him to her, her fingers in his hair.

When she pulled back from him her lips felt swollen and bruised, a sensation that she had never experienced before. 'Show me where I can have a shower, please,' she said huskily. Deep down she was trembling, wondering if it showed on the surface. More than anything she wanted to lie beside him, be in his arms, then sleep with her limbs entwined with his…

Fantasy and reality were two different things. Now in reality, she felt very, very shy.

In the spacious bathroom off the main bedroom he gave her a towelling bathrobe. 'Here's a toothbrush you can use,' he said. 'I'll get your orange juice. Take your time, love.'

'I like it when you call me "love",' she whispered, taking the things from him.

'I like saying it to you,' he said, smiling down at her. 'I have another bathroom, so you don't have to hurry. I'll bring the juice.'

It was wonderful to get under the jets of hot water, to shampoo her hair with Shay's shampoo, to lather her body with his soap. She was glad that he had not suggested they take a shower together. He was respecting her privacy and not presuming a spurious intimacy at this stage.

An arm appeared around the edge of the opaque shower curtain, holding a large glass of orange juice. Carefully, she took it from him, then he was gone. 'Thanks,' she called out.

It tasted so good, cool and pleasantly sweet to her parched throat. What a night it had been, she thought, a baptism of fire. After the ruptured appendix had been dealt with, they had had a man with multiple stab wounds. Usually such cases went to the larger hospitals, but it had happened locally. That had taken care of most of what had been left of the night.

Shyly she emerged later into the large bedroom that was pleasantly dim, where the curtains, of deep green velvet, were drawn against the winter scene outside. The whole room was decorated in various shades of green, making it like a bower. Her hair was still damp. She found that she was not questioning what she was doing, just going on instinct, living in the moment. It was not a conscious decision, she realized, it was just something that was happening. It was almost as though she were standing outside herself, observing her own behaviour, wondering exactly what she would do next.

Shay came in a moment later, dressed in a dark blue robe, his hair damp and slicked down. In his hand he carried a towel and a hairbrush. 'Let me dry your hair,' he said, touching her hair to feel its dampness. 'I do have a hairdryer, but this is nicer. Sit down.' When she sat on the edge of the bed, he gently put the towel on her head and began to rub it dry. The gesture was strangely intimate and loving, so that her throat felt tight and she wanted to cry and yet giggle at the same time. It had been years since anyone had dried her hair. For someone who did not trust love, he could be very tender and gentle, she was discovering. Then he brushed her hair back away from her face with soft, slow strokes of the brush, so that she closed her eyes with the pleasure of it.

'There,' he said, putting aside the towel and the brush. She opened her eyes to look at him, seeing his eyes blazing with the desire that he felt for her. 'Deirdre, do you want to be here with me…like this? I have to be sure.'

'Yes…yes. I do,' she said softly, hardly able to meet his gaze. 'But I am sort of…sort of…'

'Unrelaxed?' he offered softly.

'Yes. This isn't—believe it or not—something that is common in my experience, being here like this with a man I don't know very well. Although I do feel that I know you more than most. As I said, I do want to be here.' She sat demurely, her hands in her lap, her feet bare, enveloped in the huge robe that belonged to him, feeling small and very feminine, and cared for in a way that had eluded her for a long time. The tension of attraction between them was so intense that she wondered how she could bear it, and she swallowed the nervous lump in her throat.

'I understand,' he said.

Sitting there beside her, so close, he looked so attractive. With his damp hair smoothed down, it accentuated the angular bone structure of his face and the sensual curve of his very masculine mouth, she thought when she glanced at him quickly and away again, not wanting him to see the vulnerability in her eyes, the longing for him. Out of the corner of her eye she could see him smiling. I guess I don't fool him for a moment, she thought. He knows everything about me.

When he slipped the robe off one shoulder, to caress her skin with his warm fingers and his lips, she closed her eyes and let out a sigh, and she kept them closed when the robe came loose and she felt the cool air of the room on her skin. She held her breath as his hands smoothed over her shoulders, the sensation so exquisite that she thought she would faint. Automatically she reached for him, her arms going around his neck.

They both subsided sideways onto the bed in each other's arms and Deirdre began to laugh. It was such a relief to find that she was not awkward with him. 'This must be the breakfast that you promised me,' she teased.

Shay smiled down at her, propped on one elbow so that he could lean over her. 'Are you hungry? If you prefer toast,' he said, smiling, 'just say the word.'

She shook her head. 'I am hungry, but I know I couldn't eat anything. I…I'm too nervous.'

'You don't have to be nervous. Do you like the smell of lavender?' he asked softly, leaning over her, his lips inches away from hers.

'Mmm. Love it.'

He reached for a small blue bottle on the bedside table. 'I keep lavender oil here so that I can breathe in the scent of it when it seems that all the scents of the operating rooms are still in my nostrils,' he said.

'I wish I'd thought of that.' She laughed.

She watched him while he poured some of the oil into the palm of his hand and then smoothed it over her shoulder. Her eyes closed of their own volition as the lovely, delicate scent of the lavender filled her nostrils and she felt herself relaxing. 'Mmm…that's wonderful,' she murmured. When she was lying full length on the bed, he eased the robe from her.

Moments later she felt Shay's hands moving warmly, sensually over her back as she turned over onto her stomach, the lavender oil making her skin smooth and supple under his touch.

For a long time his hands moved over her, from her shoulders down over her hips, smoothing away her aches and ten-
sions, kneading the muscles and stroking her skin so that it
felt like silk, while the scent surrounded her like a cocoon.

Gently he moved her over onto her back, moving his hands
slickly over her breasts, very gently, barely touching her. 'Oh,
Shay…' she whispered. His hands moved lower, over the delicate swell of her stomach. The scent felt like a drug in her
nostrils. All that mattered was the delicate movement of his
fingers on her skin.

He kissed her then, his lips moving caressingly on hers, the
weight of his body coming down on hers as his hands caressed
her. Languorously she put her arms round his neck, holding
him against her. As he had said, she did not have to be nervous. A peace moved over her, a wonderful sense of being
loved, albeit in the arms of a man who did not trust love, the
'twenty-four-seven man'. At that moment he was very much
with her, giving her his full attention. That was all that mattered. I love you, she wanted to say, but she kept silent.
Sufficient unto the day…

'Darling…love,' he said. His arms wrapped round her,
holding her to him.

With her eyes closed, she gave herself up to him.

CHAPTER EIGHT

THAT was how it started, how Deirdre became Shay's lover, entering a new stage in her life.

Later that day, after they had both slept, he returned to work and she went home to her parents' house and prepared supper for Mungo and Fleur, inviting Fiona to have the meal with them, too.

'I want to catch up on news,' she said to Fiona on the telephone. 'I feel I haven't seen you all for ages, although it's not really long. It's strange, working through the night again.'

'I'll be there,' Fiona said. 'I spoke to my lawyer again today about giving you custody of the children, and he said again it would be better if you were married, and I told him that by the time I die you probably will be married, as I don't intend to die just yet.' Fiona laughed. 'Although I know one of the poets said that man proposes, God disposes.'

'That's often the case,' Deirdre agreed, feeling a familiar stab of anxiety about what would happen to the children if she did not get custody and Fiona became ill with a chronic illness. She would force herself to look on the bright side and hope for the best, as her mother would say. Somehow she wasn't always very good at doing that. Perhaps she was too much of a realist.

'The lawyer is also concerned that the man you marry might not want the children,' Fiona went on. 'Is there anyone, Deirdre, whom you want to marry? Someone you haven't told me about?'

'Well,' she began, blushing deeply, glad that Fiona could not see her, 'there is a doctor at the hospital—the kids have met him—whom I really like. He's divorced and, unfortunately, marriage isn't a top priority for him. He's told me that he doesn't trust love. Those were his words.'

'Well, dear, you will have to show him otherwise,' Fiona said, as though it were the easiest thing in the world. 'When can I meet this man? I might be able to drop a few very subtle hints.'

'We could all have dinner together soon,' Deirdre said. 'But, please, don't drop any hints, because they might backfire. He has a son, about the age of Mungo, give or take a few months. He's a good father, from what I've seen, and he's good with Mungo and Fleur.'

'He's the one you spent Boxing Day with? I remember now.'

'Yes, that's right.'

'Better and better,' Fiona said.

'Please, don't…er…'

'Put my foot in it? I know, dear,' Fiona said. 'I can be very tactful and subtle when I have to be, don't you worry. See you this evening.'

After her conversation with Fiona, Deirdre called Mungo and told him of their plans. He always switched on his mobile phone between classes. That night she would have supper at home and sleep in her own bed, and they would be in the house with her. 'I'll pick you up from school,' she told Mungo. 'Usual place.'

'OK,' Mungo said. 'We've missed you, Dee.'

'I've missed you, too.'

Today she felt different. This was the first day of her life after becoming Shay's lover. Unreservedly, it was the best thing that had ever happened to her and she could not get him out of her mind. Already they were planning when they could be together again. Every moment she longed for his company. Being in love was an obsession. What they had shared was a passion that had increased her love to such a point that she felt she could not live without him. Indeed, it was a kind of madness and she knew that she must try to put it into perspective. Maybe this was the very thing that he did not trust. For that reason, she was not about to tell him how she felt.

At the moment she was superbly happy, obsessed by him. 'I'd be lying if I said I could offer you a future,' he had said. It was necessary for her to keep that in mind, as well as to remind herself that it had not been very long ago that she had sat on a bus, overcome by depression. That brought the feeling that she must not run before she could walk, yet the desire to be with Shay was overwhelming her.

It would be good to have a family dinner with the kids and Fiona. She went into the kitchen to get ready for it. Tonight she was off duty and someone else would do the night shift to replace the sick nurses, then, if she was still needed, she would work on Wednesday night. The head nurse would call her in plenty of time, so that she could plan her life.

Fiona arrived not long after Deirdre had brought the children home from school.

'I want to help you prepare the food, dear,' she said. 'And I want to hear all about your job.'

'All right,' Deirdre said, preceding her into the kitchen. 'I've done most of the preparation, but you can help me serve.'

After the main course, when they were on dessert—a chocolate cake that she had made herself—the doorbell rang.

'Shall I go?' Mungo offered, rising to his feet. 'I'm good

at getting rid of canvassers and people trying to sell things. I tell them that my parents are out and I don't have any money.'

'All right,' Deirdre said.

Moments later they heard conversation and laughter coming from the front hall. 'Hey, guess what?' Mungo said, coming back into the dining room, grinning from ear to ear. 'It's Dr Melburne and Mark. They were just passing and thought they would say hello. Shall I invite them in for dessert, Dee? There's lots of chocolate cake left.'

Deirdre rose to her feet, momentarily flustered. 'Yes…' she said. 'Yes.'

'Oh, that's great!' Fleur chipped in. 'I'll get some extra plates. And shall I put the kettle on for coffee?'

'Yes,' Deirdre said, bemused and somewhat agitated. 'Bring in the cups and saucers, Fleur, please.'

Fiona rose to her feet as well, giving Deirdre a meaningful look. 'Is this the one?' She mouthed the words in an exaggerated fashion, so that Deirdre felt a desire to laugh as happiness swamped her again.

'Mmm,' she said.

Fiona appeared to gird herself up mentally, and Deirdre wanted to laugh hysterically because Fiona looked deceptively fragile, with her white hair, blue eyes and skin like old apples. Dressed elegantly in a long wool skirt and a cashmere sweater in a light lavender colour, with a string of pearls around her neck, she looked every inch a grand old lady, her fingers laden with precious rings—her weakness. 'Well, I'm so lucky to get to meet him so soon,' she whispered. 'I'll see what I can do.'

'Oh, no, don't—' Deirdre began, then was silenced by the appearance of Shay and Mark at the door of the dining room, being ushered in by the delighted Mungo. Mark was also grinning, so that Deirdre wondered if he had instigated the visit rather than his father. No matter, it was wonderful to see them.

'Come in,' she said. 'Have some cake and coffee with us. It's good to see you.'

'Thank you,' Shay said. 'I hope we're not intruding. This was Mark's idea.'

'No, you're not intruding,' she said, flushing, wondering if there were vibes from her so that the others could tell how she felt about Shay. 'Shay and Mark, this is Fiona McGregor, my employer and the children's grandmother.'

There were smiles and handshakes.

Fleur came in with some cups on a tray, wobbling it slightly. 'Hi, Mark,' she said. 'Great to see you. Come and have some chocolate cake.'

Fiona went to the kitchen to make coffee while the others sat down at the table. Soon the children were talking about what they were doing at school. Shay smiled at Deirdre, a look that made her heart feel as though it were turning over.

'And where did you meet Deirdre?' Fiona said innocently to Shay, when she was back at the table with a silver coffee-pot full of hot coffee that gave off a very appetizing aroma. Presiding over the table, she poured the liquid into cups.

'That's a long and complicated story,' Shay said, and then Deirdre knew that he could keep a confidence and had no intention of divulging anything to Fiona, as obviously she, Deirdre, would have told her herself by now. That seemed to be his reasoning, Deirdre thought.

'We met at the Stanton Memorial Hospital,' Deirdre said, which was true after all.

'That's rather mundane,' Fiona said airily, 'but it means that you have a shared interest. Coffee, Dr...er...Melburne?'

'Yes, please. And call me Shay, please.'

'That's an unusual Gaelic name,' Fiona said. 'It goes well with Deirdre and Fiona.'

'Fiona..."fair one",' Shay said.

'Appropriate once upon a time,' Fiona said, and Deirdre could see that she was charmed by Shay, while making an effort to be sharp, to suss him out.

'You must be curious to know all about me,' he said, disarming Fiona right away.

'Well…' Fiona said, laughing, 'Deirdre is like a daughter to me, as well as a very valuable employee and mother to my grandchildren, so I like to know who has an interest in her, you might say—just in case someone was planning to take her away from me, or something like that.'

Deirdre felt her face turn hot and she wondered if she could make an excuse to leave the table for a few minutes. The three children were sitting at one end of the table, their heads together, spooning forkfuls of cake into their mouths while talking at the same time.

'More cake?' she said to Shay.

'I haven't had any yet,' he said. 'I will have some.'

She half rose and cut him a generous slice, taking her time to put it on a plate.

'You are right to be anxious,' Shay said slowly to Fiona, fixing her with a speculative stare. 'She is a very lovely and unusual young woman. She's just waiting to be plucked, you might say.'

Mungo and Fleur, who had been pretending not to be listening, turned to stare at Shay, their eyes going to Deirdre and Fiona as well.

'It's all right,' Deirdre said to them, laughing, while her face felt hotter, 'I'm not about to be plucked like a ripe plum off a tree. More cake, kids?'

'Yes, please,' Mark said, tactfully rescuing her. 'Could we take it into the sitting room, Deirdre?'

'Sure,' she said.

'What's this about plucking?' Fiona said when they had gone, getting straight to the point.

'Just a manner of speaking,' Shay said smoothly. 'One day she will be gone. It's human nature.' He was smiling, and they smiled back.

Deirdre could see that it took Fiona a great effort not to ask him point-blank if he was intending that himself. Instead, she reached forward and replenished his coffee.

'Thanks. I'm an average sort of guy,' he said to Fiona, 'with no very obvious vices, except the one of working too much, although I'm better where that's concerned than I used to be.'

'Why?' Fiona said.

'Divorce,' he said.

'Oh. That's a good reason to change. Although it is rather too late.'

When Fiona went out to get more coffee and the two of them were alone, there was a tension between them that was almost tangible, and when Shay put his hand over hers as it rested on the tablecloth, she felt his touch suffuse her with an unbearable longing. The warmth of his hand tingled through her. 'Could I come back later,' he said quietly, 'to be with you for a while? I want to be with you so much. Is that possible? After the kids have gone to bed? For an hour or two.'

'All right,' she said, nodding.

'I'll call you on your mobile,' he said quickly. 'I have someone sleeping over at my apartment with Mark, so he won't be alone.' He squeezed her hand, then let it go, just as they heard Fiona coming back. 'I'm burning up, wanting to be with you.'

'Excuse me.' Deirdre left the room then, going to the bathroom to splash cold water on her face and to wash her hands, which she saw were trembling. Already she was in a situation where she could not resist him, where she longed for him constantly. The thought of being with him later, in her own small bed in her own room, filled her with agitated anticipation, so that she hardly knew what to do with herself. Absently she raked a brush though her hair and stared at herself in the bathroom mirror, at her eyes that were wide and expectant, nervous and soft with the love she felt for him. Maybe it was obvious to others as well.

When she had calmed down she went back into the dining room and found Fiona and Shay in conversation about Scottish poetry. Fiona had been a teacher of English literature during her working life.

Shay stood up. 'We must go,' he said. 'Thank you again for your hospitality.'

There were handshakes all around again at the front door as they departed.

'He's really lovely,' Fiona said thoughtfully a few minutes later when she helped Deirdre clear up and stack crockery in the dish washer. 'His ex-wife lost a good man there.'

'She used to call him the twenty-four-seven man, so he told me, because he worked such long hours,' Deirdre said.

'I can imagine it,' Fiona said. 'It's not easy to live with, but unfortunately that's what you get when you marry a doctor. They have to put some perspective in their lives, otherwise the job takes over. Hang onto him, if you can. I got the impression that he's besotted with you.'

Deirdre laughed. 'Oh, go on!' she said.

'I'm serious.'

'I wish you were right,' she said wistfully.

'I think I am right.'

'He doesn't tell me that,' Deirdre said pointedly. She knew that he wanted to sleep with her, but there might not be anything else to it.

'Do you love him?' Fiona asked.

'Oh, yes. Madly. I'm frightened of getting hurt, but I think

I'm more frightened of not allowing myself to be in a position to get hurt.'

'You mean you're going to jump in at the deep end where he's concerned?' Fiona said.

'Yes, that's just it,' Deirdre said.

'Good for you. And good luck to you.'

Deirdre thought of Fiona's words when she quietly opened the door to Shay at half past ten, when the house was quiet, the children asleep and the cat curled up in her basket in the kitchen.

He took her in his arms and kissed her as soon as the door was closed, then she took his hand and led him to her room, which was on the ground floor, away from the other two bedrooms. Very quietly she closed the door of her room until the latch clicked into place and then she turned the key in the lock.

'God, I want you.' Shay breathed the words in her ear as he held her tautly against him. He kissed her forehead, her cheeks, her closed eyelids, then her mouth, as his hands slid down over her hips, pulling her against him.

She had had a bath and washed her hair, and the delicate scent of her perfume filled the small space of her room as he slipped her dressing-gown off her shoulders so that it fell to the floor with a soft sound like a sigh. Only the thin silk of her nightdress separated her skin from the touch of his hands, and she took in a sharp breath as he smoothed his hands over her breasts, the touch making her weak with longing.

They did not want to talk much, so as not to wake Mungo and Fleur. Silently he lifted the nightdress over her head and then buried his face in the curve of her neck, holding her naked body against him. He was shaking, she could feel it, and she felt humble, aware of an answering trembling within herself, of anticipation. Quickly he undressed beside her.

When they came together, skin against skin, she let out a small moan of longing. 'Shay, Shay…I'm so glad you came back,' she whispered.

'So am I,' he said.

They lay on the bed, where she had folded back the covers to expose the cool linen sheets.

As before, he took care that she would not become pregnant, which was just as well as she did not take the contraceptive pill. Urgently they came together and she welcomed his weight on her. 'I can't get enough of you,' he said. 'I can't get you out of my mind.'

Blissfully happy, she gave herself up to him. When the swell of passion was over, they lay satiated in each other's arms, side by side.

'I love you, Shay,' she said softly, unable to constrain herself. 'I love you so much.'

For a few moments he did not say anything, then he said soberly, 'That's a pity. I wish you wouldn't.'

'Why?' she said, a shadow coming over her happiness, a foreboding.

'Because I can't promise you anything,' he said, as he stroked her hair and explored the contours of her face with his fingers in the darkness of the room as she lay warmly against him. She could not see his expression, could only sense a tension in him. 'As you know, my reputation for permanence is not good.'

'I wouldn't say that. Anyway, I'm not asking for anything permanent. I'm not asking for anything except to be with you once in a while,' she said, searching for the words with which to explain herself adequately. 'You don't have to promise me anything.'

'You're very sweet,' he murmured softly, his lips against her ear, sending tremors of awareness through her.

'Am I? I can't help loving you,' she said. 'Just accept it as a fact, Shay. You don't have to do anything about it. I…just want you to know. Did you think I could make love to you like this without being in love with you? If you think that, you don't know much about women.' As she lay there beside him, in the warmth of his arms, she felt that he was slipping away from her, at the same time that she basked in the afterglow of their love-making. 'At least,' she added thoughtfully, 'not the average, everyday sort of woman, who is not trying to trade herself off for something. There are those women, I admit. I've known some of them. I'm an average, every-day woman, someone who can be hurt. I…don't think I'm capable of trading myself. So…you see…you don't have to think of it as some sort of transaction. I shall remain an independent being and think for myself. I trust what I feel, Shay, even if you don't trust what you feel.'

'Perhaps I don't know much,' he said.

'I can't not say it, I can't pretend that I don't care,' she said, 'that it's all just physical.'

Shay pulled her head against his neck and stroked her hair. 'Don't try to analyse it,' he said. 'Just let it be for now.'

'All right,' she said softly, enjoying the closeness and the feel of him in her arms.

'I'm obsessed with you, my love,' he said. 'It must have been fate that brought you across my path.'

'Maybe it was,' she whispered back, not wanting to question out loud why he called her 'my love', when he did not love her. Perhaps it was just another expression to him, like 'sweetheart'. As he said, why try to analyse it? What she did know was that something marvellous and remarkable had happened to her in knowing him.

'Let's just live for the moment,' he said. 'Don't question it.'

'I still love you, all the same,' she murmured. 'Don't forget that.'

When he had gone and she lay curled up cosily in her bed, missing him, she thought of everything they had said. It was unsettling that he had said 'I wish you wouldn't' when she had told him that she loved him. It seemed cold and matter-of-fact somehow, even though she knew he was not a cold person but a warm and loving one. Now she wanted to cry, yet fought back the feeling. For now she would just accept the situation as it was. The need to explain herself to him had prevented her from keeping silent. Now that she had explained herself, perhaps they could just accept each other for what they were for the moment.

Perhaps he was right, that they should just live for the moment. After all, one could not force the future. And she did not have much idea of what the future held for her. That he did not love her in the way that she loved him was perhaps not important. He wanted to be with her, was obsessed by her, as he put it. With that thought, she drifted into sleep.

CHAPTER NINE

THE next days, and then the weeks, seemed to go by like greased lightning for Deirdre. With work, her home life, looking after the children, being with Shay as much as possible, trying to have a social life, going to see the counsellor, she felt like a juggler who was keeping a lot of balls in the air. Sometimes she felt that if she were to drop one of them, all the others would come tumbling down as well. Yet her mental state was lifting.

Jerry came and went in the course of his business, while she kept a low profile where he was concerned and did not breathe a word about Fiona's business and the question of the future custody of the children. Most of the time she, Deirdre, hoped that the situation would not arise in which she would have to take over custody of the children before they reached the age of eighteen. Since children of sixteen could leave home of their own free will, and a parent was not legally obliged to support a child over the age of sixteen, perhaps a nasty confrontation with Jerry would never arise.

Their cleaning lady, Alice Brenner, who had been with them for years, did a lot to keep the two homes in order to make it possible for Deirdre to work without being too anxious about the home front.

Nonetheless, Fiona continued to hope that Deirdre would marry, and that she would marry Shay. At this, Deirdre merely smiled and did not, of course, breathe a word to Shay or to the children. Fiona stated flatly that she was going to put Deirdre in her will as the guardian of Mungo and Fleur, even without official consent. No doubt Jerry would go on trying to get his hands on some of the money that Moira had left to the children. That was nothing to do with her, Deirdre felt. She didn't even want to know about it. That was something between Fiona and Jerry and their respective lawyers. Jerry's neglect of the children made life easier for all of them, in a perverse way.

As the days went by, Mungo and Fleur saw quite a lot of Mark, who often visited with Shay, and gradually it seemed that they were all one family, although no one said anything to that effect. The last thing Deirdre wanted was for Shay and Mark to feel that she wanted to take them over in some way. The cues had to come from them. Certainly, they got along well together and liked each other's company very much. They went snowshoeing and skiing together in the mountains, as well as to concerts and events in the city. Very gradually, it seemed to her, the Melburnes were coming to like her a lot and to trust her. Mark had as much reason to distrust love as his father did.

Deirdre got into the habit of talking and listening to Mark, drawing him out about his concerns. 'I've written to my mother,' he told her one day, rather shyly, 'and told her how much I miss her and wish she would come back here.'

'Did she...did she reply?' Deirdre asked, feeling an odd sensation of fear, even though she had suggested to him that he should write such a letter. If Antonia came back, what would that do to her relationship with Shay, if anything? It was impossible to think that the beautiful Antonia did not still mean something to Shay, in spite of his remarks that there was nothing left of his feelings for her. Perhaps that was the best thing that could happen, because it would give him a better idea of what he wanted, what he really felt about her, Deirdre.

'She hasn't actually sent me a letter back yet,' Mark said. 'She tends to send me little presents a lot, and just puts a card inside. I'm waiting for a proper letter.'

Deirdre swallowed to try to dispel the nervous lump in her throat. Since she had advised Mark on that course of action, she had fallen more and more deeply in love with his father, had become involved in his life in such a way that she was beginning not to be able to remember what her life had been like without him in it.

'It's good to be honest, I think,' she said to Mark. 'You've told her what you really feel.'

'If she comes,' Mark said, blushing, 'I don't think it will make a difference to you and Dad, because I think he loves you, Deirdre. She will really be coming for me.'

'I don't know whether he loves me,' she said, realizing as she uttered the words that a certain sadness had come through in her voice. 'He doesn't say so.'

'Oh, you could say that Dad's a dark horse,' he said.

Deirdre had to laugh. 'I'll take your word for it, Mark. You've known him longer than I have.'

'I'll let you know if she's coming,' he said.

She wanted to hug him. There was again a certain wistfulness in his voice. 'I hope for your sake that she does come, Mark,' she said truthfully. Whatever it did to her and Shay, it was something that had to be confronted.

Towards the end of February, which was raw, wet and dark, as was common on the west coast of Canada, Deirdre found herself working with Shay on a Friday.

'Can you come for a quick drink?' he asked her at the end

of the operating list, as he removed his face mask and his cotton operating cap outside the operating room where she was washing her hands at the scrub sinks.

'I'd like to,' she said, desperate to spend some time alone with him. 'I'll have to call Mungo and Fleur to let them know what I'm doing.'

'We won't take long,' he said. 'I have something I want to discuss with you.'

'All right,' she agreed, sensing a tension in him, an odd note in his voice. Perhaps he had heard from Antonia. Maybe she had set a definite date for coming back. Trying to hide her alarm, she smiled tentatively.

'Meet me down in the lobby,' he said. 'I know a little bar where there won't be many other people at this time.'

Deirdre nodded. 'Give me twenty minutes,' she said.

It was raining when they emerged from the hospital into the street. Shay put up a large black umbrella and drew her in beside him, keeping his arm around her shoulders. 'The bar's in a side street, within walking distance, if you don't mind walking.'

'No, I need the fresh air,' she said. Indeed, it was good to feel the cold, moist air on her face after spending the day in the artificial atmosphere of the operating suite where the incoming air was carefully filtered and warmed, before being sucked out again by the powerful ventilation system.

Resisting the urge to ask him what he wanted to talk to her about, she relaxed and enjoyed the feel of his arm around her, his warm closeness, like a bulwark against the chill of the late afternoon. It still seemed like a miracle that he should be with her, that she was with a man she loved. Sometimes in the near past she had thought that it would never happen to her, that she was not destined to find that sort of love. At that moment, the fact that he did not love her did not seem as important as the fact that she loved him.

The bar/café was cosy and warm, the sort of place with nooks and crannies where one could be private.

'Hello, Dr Melburne,' the bartender called out. 'Nice to see you again. How are you?' He was middle-aged, welcoming as he wiped the already spotless oak bar. 'Rotten day, eh?'

'Sure is.'

'How about a nice hot toddy, Dr Melburne? I make a good one with brandy and a bit of honey. Or you can have whiskey.'

'That sounds good,' Shay said, smiling at him as they both shrugged out of their coats and put the dripping umbrella into the can provided for the purpose. 'Deirdre?'

'Brandy would be good,' she agreed. 'Please, go easy on the spirits, as we're both driving.'

'Sure,' the barman said. 'It will be mostly hot water. Don't want any accidents, especially in rush hour. You find yourselves some seats and I'll bring it to you.'

'Thanks,' Shay said, taking Deirdre's arm and steering her to a corner near a window, where they were out of sight of the bar and could look out to the street where the rain sparkled in the light from streetlamps that were already on against the winter gloom. There was a small table and two chairs. There were no other customers. Soft music played in the background, enough to drown out their murmured conversation.

'Did you get through to the kids?' Shay asked. Sensitive to nuance, Deirdre sensed a tension in him and felt herself tense up as well.

'Yes. They'll go to my place from school, then I'll meet them there.'

'Good,' he said.

'What did you want to talk to me about?' she asked, unable to bear the tension any longer.

'I'll explain when we've got out drinks,' he said. 'Don't want to be interrupted.'

'Oh, dear,' she said, looking at him fully in the face, 'that sounds rather ominous.'

At that moment their drinks arrived, in glasses with handles. 'Enjoy!' the bartender said.

'Mmm, this is delicious,' Deirdre said, after sipping the hot liquid that was delicately flavoured with brandy and honey. 'I could get seriously addicted to this.'

'It is good,' he said, drinking a little then placing his glass carefully on the table in front of him. 'Deirdre...you know that Mark has written to his mother, asking her to come home? Mark said something about having told you.'

'Yes, he did say something...' Her heart gave a lurch, signalling her fear. Perhaps he was going to tell her that Antonia was back, that they had decided to get together again, to try to make a family life for the sake of their son. She looked down at the table, at her hand cupped around the glass of hot liquid, realizing again at that moment that although Shay had become a central part of her life, he could easily be out of it, that she had no claim on him. How would she manage without him? That thought came to her as though the words had been spoken aloud.

'I doubt that she'll come,' he said, the words making Deirdre realize that she had been holding her breath, waiting to hear what he would say next. Slowly, deliberately she took another sip from her glass.

'Why wouldn't she come?' she said at length. 'I understand that she wanted Mark with her...that she loves him.'

'That's true,' Shay said carefully. 'But she is with that guy, the sheep farmer. Presumably she loves him, too. I have custody of Mark, so if she wants to be in his life she has to be here. Mark could visit her out there, but so far he's declined.'

There was a silence that became uncomfortable. She took a deep breath and let it out on a sigh, trying to find the courage to say something that was appropriate. 'And you?' Deirdre asked, not looking at him, fiddling with her glass as it sat on the table. 'What will that mean to you?'

And what will it mean for me? she wanted to ask, but found that she could not utter those words, because he had always made it clear that he could not promise her anything.

'I don't know,' he said. 'For Mark's sake I would be glad, I think, if she were to come, because he needs to see her, to sort out how he feels about her, what he wants to do in relation to her. It's between the two of them. For myself, I really don't want to have to deal with her in my life again, even on the periphery. If she were to have any sort of relationship with Mark, I would, of course, have to deal with her, if only on a superficial level. I've never denigrated her in Mark's eyes, and I won't in the future.'

Deirdre swallowed to dispel the tightness in her throat. 'Mmm. I see,' she said.

For a while they sipped their drinks in silence, glad of the hot liquid, while Deirdre thought about what he had said and they both looked out of the window at the rain that pelted down on the tarmac of the road. It provided a diversion. Deirdre felt slightly sick with tension.

'Do you...still care for her?' She forced the words out. Although she had asked him that before, she felt that things had shifted enough to warrant a repeat of the question. 'Because if you do, I don't think I should be seeing you in the way that we are...'

'No, I don't care for her,' he said.

The warming effect of the drink, coupled with his emphatic assertion, had a calming effect on Deirdre, yet the underlying anxiety and longing were still there. There was nothing she could do, she decided, except to wait and see what happened. Antonia might never come, although she hoped for Mark's sake that she would. It was all mixed up in her mind.

'There's something else I want to say to you…ask you,' Shay said, fixing her with his intent grey stare, so that she could not look away. 'To perhaps solve the dilemma of what would happen to Fleur and Mungo if Fiona were to die before they reach the age of independence. I've thought that we could marry, to increase, perhaps, your chances of getting custody. And Mark needs a mother because I doubt that Antonia would leave her man in New Zealand, even if she were to come here for a visit.'

They stared at each other across the narrow expanse of the table, Deirdre's eyes wide with shock. 'You mean…' she managed, 'a sort of…marriage of convenience?'

'If you want to put it that way,' he said evenly.

'I…I don't know how else to put it,' she said. 'You don't love me.'

'No. But I do enjoy your company very much, and I want you more than I could possibly say. You're more attractive to me than any other woman has ever been.'

'That's a sort of backhanded compliment,' she said, astounded.

'Honest,' he said.

'But you don't love me,' she found herself repeating. 'And marriage is a very serious business. I don't have to tell you that.'

'No, you don't,' he said.

'I don't know what to say,' she said, twisting her hands together tightly under the table, while a strange kind of happiness gripped her as she stared at him, met his unwavering regard. Yet he did not love her…

'It would be for the children…and for us. I want to be with you,' he said. 'That's something I'm sure of.'

'I would like to say yes, Shay, but I don't know…I don't know,' she said uncertainly. 'It's so unexpected…'

'Don't wring your hands,' he said, reaching forward across the table. 'Hey, give me your hands.'

Warmly he held her restless hands in his.

'There's so much to consider…other people…' she said. 'If I had just myself to think of, I would say yes. But perhaps then you wouldn't be asking me. I'm not sure about that.'

'As I said, I want to be with you. As for love,' he said quietly, 'I have a very good and wise colleague at the hospital, whom I also count as a friend, who's East Indian, from a culture where marriages are arranged. He told me once, when I asked his advice about something personal, that in his culture you do not marry the person you love, you love the person you marry. I liked that. That's at least as good as the other way.'

'There's no guarantee that it would happen,' she said, still holding his gaze, feeling that someone had winded her. 'And…you might meet someone else whom you fall in love with.'

'There are no guarantees about anything,' he said. 'That's something I've found out.'

Deirdre did not have anything to say to that, because she knew it was true. Realizing it, though, left a feeling of something like apprehension. How good it would be if one could be absolutely certain of another person. Things changed, time moved on.

'Perhaps it's a measure of our maturity when we realize there are no guarantees, but that doesn't mean that you cannot work for something you want, something good with another person, something that you can commit to and do your damnedest to make work,' he said, gripping her hands and looking into her eyes.

The bartender came back. 'Can I get you anything else?' he asked.

'I'd like a cup of coffee, please,' Deirdre said, feeling in need of some caffeine to make sure that the alcohol had not affected her judgement.

'Sure thing. And for you, Dr Melburne?'

'Yes, the same, please, Joe.'

'Does Mark know about this?' she whispered, when the waiter had gone.

'No.'

'And what about you being the twenty-four-seven man?' she asked.

'I'm trying very hard not to be that,' he said soberly. 'I hate that term.'

They sat at the table silently, waiting for the coffee. Deirdre's heart was pounding. Whatever she had been expecting, it had not been this.

The coffee was good and Deirdre gulped at hers, wanting to counter any effect of the brandy.

'Well?' he said.

Perhaps if he had leaned across the table to kiss her, she might have accepted there and then. As it was, the warmth of his hand on her free hand suffused her with emotion. There was so much to sort out.

The tension in him was evident as he looked at her with a frown between his brows. Love for him, her need of him, threatened to overwhelm her…yet she had to be sensible, had to think this out very carefully, because it also affected Mungo and Fleur. Her chances of finding someone else who would accept her with two children who were not her own were not great.

'I'd like to think about it, Shay,' she said, forcing herself to say it, even though she wanted to tell him that she would accept him unconditionally. 'I will have to discuss it with the kids—you appreciate that?'

'Yes, of course,' he said. 'I do understand. I get impatient sometimes when I've made up my mind what it is that I want.'

Each occupied with their own thoughts, they sat silently to finish the coffee. Deirdre felt a sense of elation, yet a sense of unreality at the same time. There were times in life when you had to take the plunge, because there were no perfect times. It was just that some times were better than others. It was like having a baby, she surmised. You could wait for the perfect time then find that it never came, or that you were, after all, infertile.

Out in the rain again, under the umbrella, they linked hands to walk back to the hospital parking lot and their respective cars.

'Don't keep me waiting too long, Deirdre,' he said, as they stood beside her car.

'I'll try not to,' she said. They kissed goodbye.

'I'll see you on the weekend. I'm on call, but hopefully there will be time,' he said. 'Mark wants to get together with Mungo and Fleur, probably at your place, if that's all right with you?'

'Yes, they did ask me,' she said. 'Goodnight, Shay.'

'Goodnight, sweetheart.'

When he had walked away and she sat in her car, trying to calm her thoughts, while the rain pounded on the roof, she wondered whether the love of one person was enough for two people. Could she live with what Shay had to offer on a personal level? And would it be wise?

You don't marry the person you love, you love the person you marry—how good that sounded. Something to think about. Perhaps it was a promise of sorts, otherwise why would he have told her about it?

With that in mind, she started the engine, turned on the windshield wipers and moved out.

'That means Mark would be a sort of brother to us!' Fleur said delightedly later as they sat at supper in Deirdre's parents' house. 'Does that mean we could all live together?'

'I haven't got as far as thinking about where we would live,'

Deirdre said tiredly. 'I expect it would mean that, unless Jerry made trouble. I expect Granny would be happy with that arrangement. Remember, I haven't said yes yet.'

It had been a hectic day in one way and another. Before coming back to her own house, she had gone to Jerry's house to check up on it, to make sure that the light timers were functional, that the burglar alarm was on, even though both Fiona and the cleaning lady checked up on it as well.

She had decided to tell Mungo and Fleur while she had them as a captive audience at the dinner table. So far, so good.

Mungo gave a slow smile and looked at her knowingly. 'Is it what you want, Dee?' he said. 'You must think of what you want, not what would be best for us.'

Deirdre returned his smile. 'I think it is what I want,' she said. 'It takes some getting used to the idea, and there are a lot of practicalities to sort out. It's something that you can't rush into.' As she said those words, she wondered why Shay was in such a hurry to have her answer.

It was impossible to tell these two eager young people that Shay did not love her. For them, love would be a prerequisite. But she also knew that love and attraction were not necessarily enough. Perhaps too much was made of them. There had to be genuine willingness, she felt instinctively, to have the other person's interests at heart, on a par with your own. There had to be room in the relationship for each person to become the person they wanted to become. Perhaps the practical considerations that Shay had put forward were very sensible. If other things were not there, you could fall out of love with someone eventually, could gradually no longer find them attractive. Perhaps that was what had happened between Shay and Antonia…the long hours of work, the loneliness.

Mungo and Fleur already knew that their granny had made Deirdre their legal guardian for the future, if need be. They also knew that the lawyer had advised that her chances would be better if she were married, should Jerry make trouble. Nothing was assured. They accepted it with the stoic matter-of-factness of the young. They had to be with someone; they had to be taken care of until they were in a position to take care of themselves, to earn a living. These days, the higher education process was lengthy.

'Mark's coming round here tomorrow,' Mungo said. 'Is it all right if we talk about it to him? I want to know what he thinks.'

'That's all right. Shay's already discussed it with Mark,' she said.

'Go for it, Dee,' Mungo said quietly. 'He's a great guy.'

'I agree,' Fleur said.

Deirdre smiled.

Later that night, when the kids were in bed and Deirdre sat on the floor of the sitting room in front of the gas fire, she tried to collect her thoughts. Absently, she stroked the purring cat. Uppermost in her mind was happiness, a strange content-ment, as the love she felt for Shay seemed like a miracle that she could never have dared hope for. Although she wanted to call him and accept, she knew that she must think things through first, all the practical things—where they would live and so on, and the fact that her love for him was not recipro-cated in the same way. Of course, he cared for her—that much was obvious when they were together—but it seemed to have more to do with a strong physical attraction.

'Ah…' She stretched out her legs in front of her on the car-pet, her feet towards the fire. It was good to have the week-end ahead of her, not to be on duty. A steady rain pattered on the roof, while strong gusts of wind buffeted the house from time to time, making the inside feel secure and safe.

To add to her feeling of strange happiness was a letter from her parents that had been waiting for her when she got to the house, to say that they were planning to come home very soon. They missed her very much and needed to come back. She still needed her parents, their wisdom and advice, their love. It had seemed very odd to her not to have her family around her, although Fiona and the kids were like family. In times of crisis you needed the people you loved, who loved you in return, unconditionally.

As though on cue, her mobile phone rang.

'Hi, sweetheart,' Shay said, his voice tired. 'I was hoping I'd find you still up. How are you?'

'All right,' she said huskily.

'I'm on call, have just finished an emergency repair of ruptured spleen about an hour ago,' he said. 'The patient's stable, nothing else doing right now, so I wanted to hear your voice.'

'I'm missing you,' she said, smiling.

'Can't live without me?' There was laughter in his voice.

'It seems like that,' she said.

'Good,' he said.

'Shay…could we become engaged?' she said impulsively, having only just thought of it. 'I like the idea of being engaged. It's a promise of sorts. I think I'm a traditional woman, in the best sense, I hope.'

Shay laughed. 'I think it's a great idea. Why didn't I think of that? Do you fancy throwing a ring in my face if you decide against marrying me?' he said.

'It's an idea,' she said, laughing. 'Although I don't think I want a ring. At least, not the usual diamond or other precious stone ring. Maybe silver and amber, something chunky but not expensive. Just so that I can remind myself what I might be letting myself in for when I look at it.'

'We'll look for one,' he said.

CHAPTER TEN

'Pass me two of the long Debakey clamps, please, Deirdre,' the surgeon said to her, not looking up as his hands were in the abdominal cavity of their patient on the operating table. 'Then I'll have a piece of tape for retraction, mounted on one of those long, angled clamps.'

'Yes,' Deirdre said, looking at her array of instruments on one of her wheeled tables that stood beside the operating table. She was the scrub nurse and had everything laid out neatly in rows and types of instruments, so that she knew exactly where everything was, and could put a hand on what was needed immediately.

It was late morning and the routine operating list of elective cases had been temporarily suspended in room one while an emergency case took precedence. They had been told that a man with a dissecting aortic aneurysm was coming in by ambulance, and the case would be theirs as they had just finished a procedure. They had rushed around getting the room ready for this emergency in which, if the aneurysm ruptured, the patient could bleed to death in minutes.

An aneurysm was an abnormal ballooning out of a small section of an artery. When it was 'dissecting', this weak area was gradually splitting open and leaking blood. Because the artery had to be clamped during the operation, cutting off the blood supply to the lower part of the body, they had to work quickly, methodically and efficiently.

Deirdre passed the clamps, then the piece of thin cotton tape used for retraction. Shay smiled at her briefly, his eyes lighting up behind his protective goggles and mask. He had been pressed into being an assistant to the vascular surgeon for this emergency, as his operating room had been taken over anyway and he could not proceed with his own operating list.

Deirdre smiled back, glad he was there, then her eyes scanned her instruments and equipment again, memorizing where everything was placed.

There was a quiet tension in the room; no one spoke unless absolutely necessary. The vascular surgeon would cut open the aneurysm with a vertical incision, now that the artery had been clamped above and below it, then a graft of synthetic material would be sewn to either end of the damaged section of the artery, to form, essentially, a new blood vessel. The walls of the aneurysm would be trimmed and sewn over the graft to protect it. They would use a very fine suture needle and a fine silk or nylon suture that was also very strong, as it had to withstand the pressure of the blood flowing through the artery.

There could be complications in this operation, as the blood supply to the lower part of the body was cut off while the major artery was clamped. Deirdre's mind ranged over these possibilities, as she prepared for the next move.

'I'll take the Dacron graft now, please,' the surgeon said, after a while. 'Give me a medium-sized one.'

The circulating nurse dropped the graft, in its sterile package, onto Deirdre's instrument table.

The operation went on steadily, as it should, with Deirdre

mounting the tiny suture needles onto suture holders for the surgeon to use in sewing the graft to the cut end of the artery. When the graft was securely sewn into position and the cut portion of the artery sewn over to protect it, the moment of reckoning would come when the surgeon released the two clamps on the large artery to allow the blood to flow once again, this time through the artificial vessel. It was a tense few moments, when they had to be sure that there was no leakage of blood from the graft. If there was leakage, it meant more sewing. Sometimes blood leaked out later, in the recovery period, in which case the patient had to be subjected to another operation to correct it. So they took great pains to assess the handiwork of the surgeon before he closed the abdominal cavity. She kept careful count of the large gauze sponges, blood-soaked, that came out of the abdominal cavity.

Just before the end of the operation, the internal telephone rang, and was answered by the circulating nurse.

'Excuse me, Shay,' she said quietly, having come over to stand near Shay. 'That's the front desk to say there's an outside call for you from your son. He doesn't want to leave a message.'

It was impossible for Deirdre not to hear what the nurse had said, as she was standing at the side of the operating table directly opposite Shay. Her heart gave a sickening lurch. Every parent dreaded getting a personal call at work from a child, as it so often was not good news.

She looked at Shay sharply, noting the sudden stillness in him for those few seconds during which he contemplated the message.

'He's still on the line?'

'Yes.'

'Please, get a number—it should be his mobile phone— and I'll call him back in about fifteen minutes. If it's an emergency, he will have to leave a message.'

'All right, Shay.'

So Mark was calling his father because something serious had happened. Family members knew not to call the hospital for any other reason. Deirdre felt frightened, her concentration on the job momentarily broken. Mark had become almost like a son to her, which he would be if she were to marry Shay. She liked him, felt protective towards him, in spite of his veneer of sophistication beyond his years, and felt a delicate maternal love flowering within her where he was concerned.

In the month that had passed since Shay had asked her to marry him, she and Shay, plus the three children, had spent a lot of time together, often sharing an evening meal at one place or another. After each occasion, it seemed to her, they felt more and more like a family.

As for Jerry, he had been away for long periods, only passing through for one or two nights. Deirdre had carefully told him nothing of her plans, of her relationship with Shay, and had asked the children not to mention it to him. As for her new job, he seemed unconcerned. So long as everything carried on as usual for him, he was not interested. If not for the fact of Moira's money, he no doubt would have sold the house, left the children with her or their grandmother, where they belonged anyway, and disappeared from their lives. Deirdre had long ago decided that she could tolerate the status quo so long as Fiona remained well.

Quickly she pulled her thoughts back to the job in hand, checked what she had to hand next to the surgeon. There would be time later for Shay to tell her what was going on with Mark. Nonetheless, the feeling of anxiety remained with her.

'I'll need a vacuum drain, Deirdre,' the surgeon said.

'Yes,' she acknowledged, picking up the drain that was on her table—it consisted of a plastic box that could be compressed to create a vacuum and form a suction when attached to tubes. One of the tubes would be placed inside the abdominal cavity through a small incision made for the purpose. This drain would siphon off excess fluid and any blood that accumulated in the cavity.

When they were about to sew up the abdominal cavity, bringing the operation to an end, the surgeon spoke quietly to Shay. 'Thanks a lot for your help, Shay. Much appreciated. If you want to leave now, we can manage from here.'

'Thanks, Doug,' Shay said, backing away from the operating table. 'I appreciated the opportunity. It's been a while since I've seen a dissecting aneurysm.'

In seconds he had taken off his blood-stained latex gloves, the nurse had undone his surgical gown for him, he had stripped it off and left the room.

Deirdre felt her anxiety level increasing, as she hoped he would come back at the end of the operation to tell her what had happened. It would be a while before she could get away herself for a late lunch. Now she was conscious of being very hungry, desperate for a cup of coffee, and had already decided to go to the hospital cafeteria for a proper meal.

There was still a lot for her and the circulating nurse to do before either of them could leave to get something to eat. In a major operation like this, with the abdominal cavity open, all the sponges, instruments and suture needles that were on the sterile set-up had to be counted twice. Before Shay departed they had completed one count; now they had to do the second count.

When Deirdre looked at the clock, she was surprised to see how much time had elapsed since she had last checked. At this rate, she would be working late, staying on to help the evening shift nurses, who were due to check in for duty at a quarter past three.

When the second count was completed, she passed the

surgeon the first suture for the sewing up. The circulating nurse gave her the thumbs-up sign, signalling that she had done a good job. It had been a long time since she had last assisted with a ruptured or dissecting aneurysm. The little knot of anxiety that had seemed to settle in the pit of her stomach at the start of the operation, over whether she could cope, dissipated now that she was on firm territory. It was replaced more clearly by a worry about Mark.

When the operation was over and the patient wheeled out on a stretcher to go initially to the recovery room, from where he would go on later to the intensive care unit, Deirdre stacked her used instruments in a bowl of water. All would be wheeled by her out to the dirty prep room, where they would be cleaned and sterilized. Now that it was finished, her concentration over, she felt fatigued. Her back ached, as well as her feet. The longing for a cup of good coffee, which she had felt for the last hour or two, translated itself into a craving now.

'Shall I go on for a lunch-break now?' she called to the circulating nurse as she wheeled her used instruments on a bowl-stand through the door.

'Sure, Dee. You must be starving. I'll set up here for Shay's next case.'

Having divested herself of the dirty instruments and other equipment, Deirdre washed her hands at the scrub sinks, took off her paper hat, ran her fingers through her hair and put on her white lab coat over her scrub suit. She would go to the locker room to change her shoes, then go down in the elevator to the lobby and on to the cafeteria.

There were several other people in the elevator, no one she knew, and they all got off *en masse* in the lobby. Deirdre found herself pushed forward with the small crowd, and as she turned to cross the lobby in the direction of the corridor to the cafeteria, she saw Shay crossing the lobby ahead of her. Her face lit up with a welcoming smile.

He did not see her, his face intent and serious as he strode towards the main entrance. From where she stood, watching him, Deirdre saw him go up to a woman who was waiting just inside the main doors. Then the welcoming smile that she had prepared for him froze on her face as she watched him take the woman in his arms and give her a hug.

Deirdre went into the gift shop and looked at the pair through the window, feigning interest in some greetings cards. The woman was, without doubt, his ex-wife Antonia. She recognized her from the photograph she had seen in Mark's room, albeit this flesh-and-blood woman was an older, more tired version of that picture. As they stood talking, standing close together, Deirdre got a good look at her as she was facing her way, while Shay had his back to her. The woman was talking, not smiling.

It seemed clear to Deirdre that Antonia had come unexpectedly back into the country from New Zealand, which was probably why Mark had telephoned his father. She suddenly felt physically sick and paralysed by indecision. Should she go out and make herself visible so that Shay would introduce her? After all, Shay had asked her to marry him, and she had agreed to become engaged. Somehow she could not do it. Her legs would not move, in the way she had felt paralysed and unable to get off the bus all those weeks ago.

The decision was taken out of her hands for the time being, as Shay took Antonia's arm and gestured towards the cafeteria, no doubt suggesting a meal or a cup of coffee. When they had gone from view, Deirdre bought herself a bar of chocolate, going through the motions automatically, stalling for time to think what to do next. From the little coffee-stall in the lobby she bought a cup of coffee.

Taking these with her, she pushed blindly through the main doors to the outside, welcoming the cold and the rain as they would keep other people away and she could be alone. For now, she felt that she desperately wanted to be alone to think. She forced herself to sip the scalding hot coffee, her appetite gone now that she felt sick.

Perhaps what she had seen meant no more than it appeared at face value. Antonia had come back to see Mark, had decided to come without informing anyone that she was coming, perhaps to assure herself that Mark was all right before anyone could arrange a neat scenario. Deirdre could imagine herself doing the same if she wanted to check up on a child. Where did that leave her? She asked herself that again. Her world, which had come to seem secure and happy, had become uncertain again, in a different way. She felt frightened that the man she loved would be overwhelmed by former loyalties and responsibilities. If you were a good parent and a decent human being, you usually did what was best for a child.

As she drank the coffee slowly and forced herself to eat some of the chocolate, the thought came to her that perhaps Shay had asked her to marry him because he had known that Antonia would eventually come back and perhaps try to reclaim her son by legal means. The letter that Mark had written to her, his mother, would perhaps provide legal ammunition if she wanted to make another bid for him.

Perhaps Shay wanted her, Deirdre, to be a mother to Mark for those reasons, to marry her so that his claim on his son would be more assured, rather in the way that Fiona had suggested to her that if she were married she would have a better chance of being a legal guardian of Mungo and Fleur in the event of Fiona's death.

The feeling of physical sickness increased as she thought about this, while it crystalized in her mind as a certainty rather than a possibility. Shay had, after all, admitted that he did not love her, that the marriage would be a marriage of convenience—'if you want to put it that way', he had said.

The dullness of the cloudy, wet day suited her mood as she stared across the street from under the shelter of the entrance overhang. Perhaps she had been naïve to think that a sophisticated, attractive professional man like Shay would be interested in her, a young woman some people would call a 'home body', the opposite of a sophisticated career-woman. Well, that was what she was. She enjoyed making a home for children, loving them, having pets, doing gardening, making a house into a home instead of a showcase where no one really felt comfortable—as she had seen in some of the homes of the kids' friends. She enjoyed family dinners, cooking for people she cared about, gathering around a table to discuss personal and world affairs alike, exchanging ideas. 'That's the way I am,' she said aloud, as tears pricked her eyes.

Was Shay using her, in his own way, in the same way that Jerry was using her to keep his home going while he was away, capitalizing on the fact that she loved the children? She did not want to think so, yet the persistent thought niggled at her, even though she tried to tell herself that the suspicion was a product of her low self-esteem.

'Don't read more into something than is there,' she muttered to herself fiercely, while the persistent tears made her eyes ache. 'Wait until you have talked to Shay.'

As she walked back across the lobby to get to the elevator once again, she tried to compose herself, repeating like a mantra the need to be fair and keep an open mind. If she had possessed a certain aplomb, she would go to the cafeteria now and pretend that she had not seen Shay and Antonia in the lobby, just walk by them so that he would have to acknowledge her presence, and the ball would be in his court. She did not have that aplomb.

Shay was due back in the operating room very soon to continue with the operating list of elective cases. This time she would be the circulating nurse while her colleague would be the scrub nurse, as they generally alternated with cases. Perhaps she would get an opportunity to tell Shay that she had seen him with Antonia. If she did not tell him right away, she could imagine that the tension between them would be unbearable.

'Will you scrub, Anne?' she asked her colleague as soon as she returned to room one.

'Yes, if you like. The patient's on his way, and we've put in a call for Shay.'

'OK,' Deirdre said, feeling calmer now that professional mode had to take over. Her private life must not intrude, yet she had every intention of saying something to Shay.

'I'll open the packs,' she added, while Anne went out of the room to the scrub sinks. She would open the sterile packs of drapes and instruments on the wheeled tables that Anne would need.

She had her back to the door when Shay came in, yet she could sense his presence, knew it was him. The pull of attraction between them was like a palpable thing.

'Deirdre,' he said, merely to acknowledge her.

She turned round to him, struck anew by how attractive he looked in his green scrub suit, his tall, masculine frame accentuated by the simplicity of the attire. Yet somehow he suddenly seemed a little more remote from her. He was tying on a face mask.

Deciding that confrontation was the best way to proceed, she said, 'I saw you in the lobby with Antonia.'

'Oh…' he said, suddenly still, his eyebrows raised in surprise.

'I…assume she came to see Mark?' she forced herself to

say calmly, while inside she wanted to shout at him to tell her what was going on. 'That neither you nor Mark knew she was coming. Otherwise you would have told me—yes?'

'Yes, on all counts,' he said quietly. 'I'm sorry you had to see her before I had a chance to explain.'

'Is that why you want to marry me?' she said bitterly, blurting the words out, not having planned to say them at that precise moment. Her anxiety was speaking for her. 'So that Antonia would have less of a chance in maybe taking Mark away…if that is what she wants to do?'

'No!' he said emphatically, as they faced each other tensely in that inappropriate setting for such a conversation. 'Legal custody has been settled.'

'That could perhaps be overturned,' she persisted. 'Mark sent her a letter saying he missed her.' She wondered if he knew that she herself had suggested such a letter to the sad boy. Some time soon she would have to bring that up. Right now, she felt tense with anxiety about her future with Shay. At the same time, she felt a grudging respect for Antonia in having, apparently, responded to her son's call.

'You have no need to be jealous,' he said astutely.

Before she could reply, the anaesthetist stuck his head round the door. 'Hi, Shay,' he said. 'Is it all systems go?'

'Yes, as far as I'm concerned,' he said. 'Deirdre?'

'Give us five minutes,' she said, turning away from Shay to get on with her work. Her throat felt tight with emotion.

'We'll talk later,' Shay said, going out.

'Can you stay late?' one of the senior nurses said to her at three o'clock. 'To help out the evening shift nurses?'

'I'm afraid I can't this time,' she said decisively, deciding in that instant. 'I have to pick up children from school.'

'I didn't know you had kids.'

'Well, I do. Sorry. Sometimes I can do it, but not today.'

That was that. She wanted to get away as quickly as possible.

Shay came up to her as she was washing her hands at the scrub sinks, as they were between cases. 'Can I see you later on tonight, to talk?' he asked. 'I could come to your place. Mark is going out to dinner with his mother, to get to know her again without my presence.'

'All right,' she agreed, her voice stiff. 'Come to my house, for supper, if you like, or afterwards if you don't have time. What does it all mean, Shay?'

'We'll talk later,' he said gently. 'For you and me, there's no change.'

'I don't quite see it that way,' she said bleakly.

It was time to go back into the room, until she was relieved by the evening shift nurses and could go to pick up the kids. His very gentleness brought a tightening of her throat again and the threat of tears to her eyes. Perhaps that was his way of hinting to her that what they had shared would soon be over, preparing her, in spite of his words to the contrary. How difficult it was to go back into that room and behave in a normal professional manner.

CHAPTER ELEVEN

WITH Mungo and Fleur in tow, she stopped at Jerry's house *en route* to her own, to find him there.

'That's Jerry's car,' Fleur said, indicating the expensive European car that was parked on the street opposite the house.

'So it is,' she said, as she parked outside the house gate, too preoccupied to worry about any sort of confrontation with him. True to her word, she had not cooked for him from the time that she had told him she would not do it any more. 'Get anything you have to pick up here, then we'll go on to my place for supper. I want to stop at a fish shop to get some seafood. You two can help me cook. Shay might be joining us for supper.'

'Great!' Mungo said. 'Will Mark be there?'

'I don't think he can come, but I'm not certain.' This was not the right moment to tell them that Mark's mother had arrived in the country.

Jerry was on the phone in the kitchen when they all trooped in, relieving them of a necessary preliminary greeting. Deirdre just raised a hand to him before starting on her round of the house to make sure everything was all right, while Mungo and Fleur went upstairs to get clothes and books. As time went by, they kept less and less there. Although it was a large, modern and convenient house, it did not seem like home to any of them. It had Jerry's stamp on it in the showy furniture and carpets that were, it seemed to her, more suitable to a mogul's palace. Even so, she never criticized it to the children. It was Jerry's taste, and that was that. It was partly his house after all. Very soon, she hoped, she would not have to be in it.

'Hi, there,' Jerry said when they came downstairs again. 'How's the family, then?' He was smiling affably, no doubt having concluded a good business deal.

'We're good,' Mungo said, with dignity. 'We're just going over to Dee's for supper.'

'OK,' he said. 'I'll be leaving for Hong Kong tomorrow night.'

'All right,' Deirdre said. 'Everything here at the house is good.'

He nodded, already distancing himself from them, distracted. 'I'll be joining friends for dinner,' he said, as though she had not told him that she was not going to cook, as though the initiative were his. 'We're going to the Clarion Hotel.'

Deirdre nodded. 'Have a good journey,' she said politely.

They filed out of the house again and into her car. 'Now for the fish shop,' she said, letting out a sigh of relief.

'Mollykins will love us for getting fish,' Fleur said.

The supper was almost ready later when Shay called to say he was on his way. Deirdre, sensitive to his tone, was aware that he was tense, and there was an answering tension in her. Perhaps something had to be resolved between them this evening.

Round her neck on a chain she wore the heavy silver and amber ring that they had chosen together from the studio of a local craftsman, which was part of their pledge to one another. It signified that although she had not exactly said she would marry him—although she longed for it—it did signify that she was holding herself aloof from others to be with him with a view to marriage, a promise of sorts. That promise could be broken, of course. It was not, she thought self-deprecatingly, that there were any others.

The ring was warm with her body heat against her skin, hidden under clothing, reminding her of her troth, if one could call it that. The warmth of it, its heaviness, were somehow re-assuring in this time of uncertainty. She liked the word 'troth', which she knew meant 'truth' in Old English. Perhaps this evening they would each speak their truth. Shay had said to her that he wanted her to have the ring, to keep it for ever, no matter what happened between them, so she had accepted it on those terms. They had discussed that they both liked amber, because it was an ancient fossil resin, from something that had once lived. Although there were imitations, the real thing was not common. Even though Shay had not said that he loved her, it signified to her a lasting love.

'Would you let Shay in, please, Mungo?' she said when the doorbell rang. 'Fleur, please help me carry the dishes into the dining room.'

'Where's Mark tonight?' Deirdre heard Mungo ask when he let Shay into the front hall.

'He's gone out to dinner with someone else,' Shay said. 'I'll tell you about it a little later.'

When she went out to greet him she was shocked to see how exhausted he looked. His face was pale and drawn as though he were tormented by mental anguish—as probably he was, she thought.

'You're just in time.' She smiled at him, forcing a lightness. 'We're about to eat.'

'I'll just wash my hands. Hi, Fleur. How are you?'

'I'm pretty good, Shay, thank you. Where's Mark?'

'That's a long story, which I'm going to tell you in a while.'

'Is he all right?'

'Sure.'

When they were all eating, Shay put down his knife and fork and spoke into the expectant silence, getting right to the point. 'The reason I didn't bring Mark with me is that he's gone out to dinner with his mother. She came back unexpectedly from New Zealand, without telling anyone except a couple of her old, close friends. She contacted Mark, then he called me at work today to tell me.'

'Geez!' Mungo said, forgetting to chew for a moment.

'Is he happy about that?' Fleur asked perceptively.

'He seemed to be,' Shay said carefully. 'The test will come tonight, after he's been alone with her for two hours or so. They always had a good relationship…'

'Why did she go, then?' Fleur said.

'It was more to do with me than Mark,' Shay said. 'I was working too much and she couldn't take it. I don't blame her for that.'

Deirdre looked down at her plate, pushing her food around. She admired him for the straightforward way he was answering the kids' questions, yet she felt she was crying inside, as though she had found herself suddenly pushed aside in Shay's life, in Mark's life. That was silly, really, because she did not have any claim on Mark…and not much on Shay, she told herself.

'Can we still see Mark?' Mungo said, giving Deirdre a quick glance. 'I mean, can we see him soon, and still be friends?'

Deirdre knew Mungo well, knew exactly what he was asking—whether the relationship between her and Shay was over with the return of his ex-wife, and thus their friendship with Mark, which they had hoped would be more than that.

'Of course you can,' Shay said. 'He wants that. My former wife, Antonia, may be going back to New Zealand…she hasn't made up her mind yet.'

Would she try to take Mark with her? That was the unspoken question hanging over them. They did not voice it, because it was clear that Shay did not know. Mark was old enough to have a say.

'Eat up,' she said to the children. 'There's apple pie after this.'

Deirdre forced herself to put a forkful of food into her mouth, chew and swallow, then another, while Shay continued to talk to Mungo and Fleur. He was a good father, she thought again, would be a good father to Mungo and Fleur, who had never known their biological father. She found herself praying that this all indeed would work out, that he would eventually be a father to them.

At this moment, Mark would be with his mother, talking, making up for lost time. Perhaps they would both find, she speculated, that too much water had gone under the bridge for them to take up where they had left off. They would have to forge a newer, more mature relationship. There might be some resentment on Mark's part, while Antonia would feel guilty for having gone, no doubt.

As Deirdre watched Shay across the table as he spoke to the children, loving him as she did, certain decisions were forming in her mind, as of their own volition.

'I'll clear up,' she said to the children when dinner was over. 'You get on with your homework.'

'OK,' Mungo said, as they both went to the sitting room where they had dumped their knapsacks of books earlier, leaving her in the cramped dining room with Shay.

'You've been very quiet,' he said quietly to her, coming over to her and putting his arms around her.

'Yes,' she said. 'I think I'm in a state of shock. The past seems to have caught up with you, Shay.'

'We never really shuffle off the past,' he said, looking down at her, his eyes holding hers so that she had to look fully at him. 'We can't just switch it off and pretend that it didn't happen, that it hasn't affected us.' He gently pulled her head against his chest, stroking her hair, and she felt tears gather in her eyes. It would be devastating to give him up, if she had to.

'We can talk in the kitchen,' she said, reluctantly breaking away from him, not wanting Mungo and Fleur to hear their personal exchange. Together they carried the dishes and plates out of the room. Always in her mind, since early afternoon, had been the image of Shay putting his arms around Antonia and hugging her. It was a simple, normal gesture between two civilized people, she told herself again. After all, he did not hate her.

'I've been thinking,' she said, turning to face him in the kitchen, 'that maybe we should not see each other until the situation has been resolved between you and Antonia—although I hope that Mungo and Fleur can still see Mark, as they would miss him, and he them.'

'And you wouldn't miss me?' he said, standing close but not touching her, his face pale and drawn.

'Of course I would,' she said, her voice trembling, 'but I can't reconcile myself to the fact that you asked me to marry you but you don't love me. Now that Antonia's here I feel that I…um…need to be more certain about things. We need time away from each other.'

'I don't feel that I do,' he said. 'I enjoy being with you.'

Deirdre found that she could not, at that moment, voice her suspicions that he wanted her to strengthen his position against his former wife, even though things seemed cut and dried legally where Mark was concerned.

'I…would like to stay away from you until Antonia either goes back to New Zealand or something else is resolved between you. I'm not a part of what you have to decide…what Mark has to decide. Does she know about me?'

'Not yet,' he said grimly.

'There you are,' she said.

'There hasn't been time to tell her,' he said. 'Her priority is Mark, not me. I'm not an issue with her. You must see that.'

'Maybe not,' she said, still facing him, feeling as though she wanted to cry. 'But that's the way it is with me, Shay. I love you…but I'm not sure of you… It has to be right…'

Mungo came in, ostensibly to get a glass of water. 'I hope you two aren't quarrelling,' he said, with the air of a wise old man.

'We wouldn't do that,' Shay said. 'We're simply discussing a few issues.'

Mungo nodded sagely, really none the wiser, and went out bearing his glass of water.

They stood looking at each other, a tension of sadness in her vying with the intense attraction to him. Just then his pager went off, as though on cue, a tinny beeping that was the sound of duty calling.

Shay took it out of his pocket, looked at the number displayed there and then switched it off. 'The hospital,' he said. 'Probably about one of my post-op patients. Could I use your phone?'

'Sure,' she said.

He pocketed the pager. 'The twenty-four-seven man,' he said cynically, with a twisted, self-deprecating smile. At that moment, Deirdre felt suddenly that she knew him better than she had before today. There were regrets in his life that she had not experienced herself, things that were not easy to live with. The phrase also served to bring Antonia somehow into the room with them, coming between them.

'It's in the nature of the job,' she said, knowing that to be true.

When it was time for him to go, she and the children stood at the door to say goodbye.

'We'll see each other at work,' she said, knowing that only

he would understand that work was the only place where they would meet now, as they had agreed that they would not see each other for a while in their free time.

Lying in bed later, restless, she felt that the bottom had dropped out of her newly created world, that she had somehow gone back to an 'as you were' situation. Yet it was not exactly like that. She had a fulfilling job now that she really liked, she was no longer a servant of Jerry, she had made decisions that had improved her life. The guardianship of Mungo and Fleur would only become an issue if Fiona died. Before long, her parents would be home.

What she wanted most in the world was still just beyond her reach.

There was a poignancy to everything she did at work after that. They worked together, talked, looked at each other longingly from a distance, it seemed. All the time, she waited for word about Antonia.

Mark came to their house several times, for supper and to hang out with Fleur and Mungo, during which time he talked a bit about his mother but did not say what she was planning. He did not seem exactly happy that she was back. He seemed more thoughtful and distracted, Deirdre judged, and yet a little more relaxed. It was as though his longing for his mother, having been assuaged, had lost its hold on him. In the meantime, Deirdre watched and waited for something to happen.

'It is ridiculous, Deirdre,' Shay said to her one hectic morning, when they stood briefly together at the scrub sinks outside room one, 'that we shouldn't be seeing each other outside work.' He looked haggard and stressed, as she often did herself these days.

'It's the best way, Shay,' she said, crying inside, wanting so much to touch him. 'It should be self-limiting.'

'Mark wants to know,' he said, 'whether we can all get together, with his mother, to have a meal at a restaurant. Would that be all right with you? I get the impression that he wants to make an announcement.'

'Yes,' she said.

She had to go then, to push their patient on a stretcher into the operating room for their first case of the day. 'We'll talk later,' she promised him, feeling that things were coming to a head with Mark and his mother, and perhaps for her and Shay as well.

A week later Deirdre, Mungo and Fleur all filed into The Joker restaurant. Deirdre, carefully dressed to look casually sophisticated, looked up at the name ruefully. That was appropriate a lot of the time for what life handed out to you. She couldn't complain. Life had been more good than bad to her over the past weeks. Her paralysing dilemmas had somehow unravelled, and she felt now that the initiative was hers with regard to whether she and Shay would be together.

Nonetheless, she felt a nauseating apprehension at meeting Antonia, forcing herself to move forward, to keep her face serene.

Mark, Antonia and Shay were already seated at a table for six when she and the children came in. As she moved towards them she thought it was appropriate that they should be here again, where Shay had brought them when she had been at her lowest ebb, where he had rescued them, so to speak. Yet here he was with his former wife, and they looked like a family. Once you had a child, she thought, you were always a family of sorts, even though the formal relationship had been dissolved.

A mixture of intense emotions occupied her mind as she went forward, with no time for her to identify them before Shay and Antonia were standing up to greet them.

'Deirdre,' Shay was saying, 'this is Antonia. Tony, this is Deirdre, Mungo and Fleur.'

They all said hello. In a daze Deirdre allowed her arm to be taken by Antonia and drawn forward to a seat beside her. 'Come and sit next to me,' Antonia said, her voice soft and her accent a mixture of Canadian and New Zealand.

Obediently Deirdre sat down, while Mungo and Fleur sat on either side of Mark, who was smiling at them, obviously very happy to have them there—his surrogate brother and sister, Deirdre thought, staring across the table at them. Shay's eyes met hers, and he seemed to be giving her the message that this was Mark's show.

A waiter having placed a menu in front of her, Deirdre turned to Antonia, looking at the tired face of the other woman, whose tanned skin was criss-crossed with fine lines around the eyes, as though she had been exposed to a lot of sun. The beautiful woman of the photograph had remained beautiful, had matured gracefully and naturally. Her blonde hair was pulled back into a delicate knot at the nape of her neck, giving her a sophisticated air.

'It's good to meet you, Deirdre,' Antonia said. 'Mark's told me a lot about you and the children…and Shay has, too.' She sounded nice—reasonable and nice.

'I can't say that they've told me a lot about you,' Deirdre said with a nervous laugh, wondering if Antonia knew that Shay wanted to marry her.

'No…well…' Antonia said softly, while the others engaged in lively conversation. 'I'm the black sheep, the breaker-up of the family. But really, you know, families break up long before the members actually leave each other. Once the emotions are disengaged, that is the real end.'

Deirdre stared at her, amazed that she should be so frank so quickly. She swallowed nervously. Could she match that?

'We haven't much time,' Antonia said, as though Deirdre had voiced her surprise. 'There isn't much point now in procrastinating about things. I'm so pleased that Mark likes Mungo and Fleur, that he talks about them as though they were his siblings. He's needed that. I suppose Shay told you that he had a problem with drugs at one point?'

'Yes,' Deirdre said, dazed.

'That seems to be over now, thank God. I've missed Mark like hell…wanted him to be with me. He knows that more fully now, I think, and doesn't blame me as much. He knows that I love him, and always will. I'm negotiating with John— that's my partner—to spend a lot of time here in British Columbia, and the rest of the time in New Zealand. He's looking into buying land here and a winery. In New Zealand he has a wine-growing business and a sheep farm, two things that he could also do here. Mark needs me around a lot for at least another five years.'

Deirdre nodded. Antonia seemed to be a very nice person. Deirdre had the feeling that Shay had lost something worth having in her. That thought elicited a sadness in her, a mourning. Perhaps that was why Shay could not love her…or could not say that he loved her. She did not know that she could be a match for Antonia. What to do? What to do?

'I hope it works out,' she said. 'I know that Mark would be happier with you in the same country, not too far away.' She forced herself to say the words, even though she did not know what those events would mean for her personally. All she knew at that moment was that the story, the ongoing saga, was not hers alone. In fact, she was on the periphery really, with no past that involved them. The absent John would also very obviously have a say. He must be an accommodating man to be willing to live in two places.

'Did Shay tell you he wants to marry me?' she finally

found the courage to say, knowing that the others were making too much noise for Shay to hear her pose the question.

'Oh, yes,' Antonia said. 'I think that would be good for him. He's a good man. I get the impression that you would be good for each other. His downfall is that he doesn't know how to balance his life. He chose the wrong woman in me, because I'm self-centred. I want a lot of things for myself, and I'm not willing to compromise beyond a certain point. I admit it freely. Don't let that happen to you, if you decide to marry him. After all, you're a long time dead.'

'I want to have children,' Deirdre found herself saying to this woman who was a stranger to her, this woman who had rejected the man she herself wanted. 'Three or four.' Oh, do you? Her alter-ego asked the question. That was something she had not discussed fully with Shay.

Antonia nodded. 'A proper family,' she said, so that Deirdre looked at her closely, seeming to hear a touch of wistfulness and regret in the other woman's voice.

The waiter came then with his notepad, and Deirdre ordered a generic meal, not bothering to peruse the menu exhaustively as her mind was churning and most of the print meant nothing to her.

'I've chosen the wine,' Shay said to her, no doubt noting her somewhat bewildered expression, she thought with a sudden desire to laugh hysterically. Her fear of meeting Antonia, thinking she might be snooty, had not been justified. Shay's ex-wife was probably more up-front than she was herself.

The food came relatively quickly, and as they ate Shay smiled at her from time to time, as though from a distance, aware as he was that Antonia had targeted her, so to speak. Hardly aware of what she was eating, Deirdre munched her way through her food, while the three young people chatted and laughed with abandon, as though they were unaware of any vibes between the adults.

When the first course had ended and they were waiting for dessert, Mark said, 'Can everyone listen, please? I have something to say that affects all of us.' He was shy and decisive at the same time as he turned to his mother. 'I love you, Mum. I'm very happy you're back and that you'll be living part of the time here, but I want you to know…and everyone to know…that I love Deirdre as well, and you two, Mungo and Fleur…and Dad. I think it's all come clear to me.'

He paused to take a drink of water, while the others at the table were silent, not moving, their eyes on him, Deirdre felt tears prick her eyes and she pressed her lips together hard to stop them trembling. Out of the mouths of babes…

'Maybe we can work something out,' Mark went on, sounding mature beyond his years, 'so that we can all see each other when we want to…find a way to be together. I'm fed up with being away a lot of the time from people I want to have in my life.'

'That sounds fair enough,' Antonia said, after a silence that was one of respect for Mark.

'Good for you, Mark,' Shay said. 'I'm proud of you, in more ways than one.'

A slow blush of pleasure coloured Mark's face, while Mungo and Fleur smiled at him. Deirdre had the feeling that the ball was in her court as she blinked away tears. With all of them working together for something good, surely it would happen.

When dinner was over and they made their way to their cars, Deirdre found herself walking with Shay, behind the others. When he gripped her hand, she did not pull away.

'For someone who doesn't trust love,' she said quietly, 'your son obviously loves you.'

'Yes,' he said. 'I thought he handled all that very well. I didn't know what he was going to say, only that he wanted to say something.'

'He did handle it well,' she agreed, her voice husky with the need to cry. The feel of Shay's warm hand on hers added to the feeling. More than anything in the world, she wanted to be with him, wanted them to belong to each other. 'What you don't trust is your own love. Is that right? Or mine? Well, I think I'm a one-man woman.'

'Still waters run deep?' he said, giving her hand a squeeze. 'I guess I sensed that when I first met you.'

Mark got into a car with his mother, after saying goodbye.

'I'd like to talk to you,' Shay said to Deirdre. 'May I come to your place? I don't think it can wait any longer. I'll follow you in my car.'

She nodded, not trusting her voice. For the first time in a long time she felt that things were, maybe, going to be all right. There were a lot of practicalities to iron out, but the main hurdle seemed to have been vaulted. 'I…like your wife,' she managed to get out, as she unlocked the door of her car.

'She's a nice person,' he agreed. 'I expect she told you that she's very focused on herself, but not in a selfish way. She knows what she wants and goes for it…and doesn't see why she shouldn't get it. She gets it herself, she doesn't expect anyone else to get it for her. And she's not my wife…keep that in mind.'

'I'm very different, I think,' she said. 'Perhaps I don't focus on myself enough.'

'Of course you're different. That's what's so great about you. You call yourself a home body…well, I admire that. You know your priorities and you have the courage to be what you want to be…a good mother, a good person.'

'Do I?' she said, surprised. 'You make me sound as though

I've got it all together, when a lot of the time I feel as though I'm made up of a lot of loose ends.'

He laughed. 'That's normal,' he said. 'You manage very well.'

'Hey, Dee,' Mungo interrupted, 'are you expecting us to walk home, or what?'

'Get in,' she said, pulling open the car door, smiling at them, wanting to hug them and Shay as well. This is my family, she thought, people I love.

Shay was right behind them when she parked her car in the short driveway of her parents' home.

'Hey, kids,' Shay called to them, 'you go on inside while I talk to Deirdre out here in private.'

'OK,' Fleur said, with great alacrity, as though she sensed that something momentous was about to happen. 'It's pretty cold out here.'

'We'll keep each other warm,' he said.

When the kids were inside and the door closed, Shay took her hand and drew her under the shelter of the covered porch.

'Will you marry me?' he said, a shadowy figure looking down at her. 'It bears repeating.'

'I…' She wanted to shout 'Yes!', but somehow the surge of emotion took away her voice.

He leaned forward and kissed her on the cheek. 'It so happens,' he said, 'that I would be marrying the person I love, and would love the person I marry—the best of both worlds.'

Deirdre took the short step forward that would bring her up close to Shay and put her head against his chest. His arms closed around her. 'I love you,' he said. 'I like you and I love you.'

She closed her eyes, unable to speak.

'Shall I go now?' he said.

'Stay,' she whispered, 'please…'

MILLS & BOON

Live the emotion

Tender romance™

THE CATTLE BARON'S BRIDE *by Margaret Way*

The wilderness of the Australian Northern territory was no place for city beauty Samantha Langdon. Cattleman Ross Sunderland wouldn't have agreed to act as guide if he'd known Sam would be on the trip – he'd vowed to avoid her. But with danger and beauty all around them, their passion could no longer be denied…

THE CINDERELLA FACTOR *by Sophie Weston*

The French chateau is the perfect hiding place for Jo – until its owner, reporter Patrick Burns, comes home… At first Patrick thinks the secret runaway is a thief, until he sees that Jo is hiding her painful past. Soon she is a woman he can't live without. But will her frightening new feelings for Patrick make Jo run again?

CLAIMING HIS FAMILY *by Barbara Hannay*

Erin has taken her little boy to the Outback to meet his father – her ex-husband, Luke – whom she hasn't seen for five years. Erin is not sure how to act around the man she once loved so deeply. Can Erin find the courage to give their marriage a second chance – and let them become a family again?

WIFE AND MOTHER WANTED *by Nicola Marsh*

Brody Elliott is a single dad struggling to bring up his daughter Molly. He's determined to protect his little girl from heartbreak again. So when Molly befriends their pretty new neighbour, Carissa Lewis, Brody is wary. If only Brody was willing to let go of his past and give in to their attraction, maybe Carissa could be his too…

On sale 5th May 2006

Available at WHSmith, Tesco, ASDA, Borders, Eason, Sainsbury's and most bookshops

www.millsandboon.co.uk

MILLS & BOON®
Live the emotion

0406/03b

_Medical
romance™

HER LONGED-FOR FAMILY by Josie Metcalfe

Doctor Nick Howell has never forgiven Libby for
running out on him – until she turns up as the new
A&E doctor and it becomes clear that an accident
and resulting amnesia has cut out part of her life.
Now it's up to Nick to help her remember...

The ffrench Doctors – a family of doctors –
all in the family way

MISSION: MOUNTAIN RESCUE
by Amy Andrews

Army medic Richard Hollingsworth has devoted
his life to saving others. But his medical skills have
put his life in danger – and that of his beloved Holly.
Now, to escape their mountain captors, they must
submit to the bond they once shared...

24:7 Feel the heat – every hour...every minute...
every heartbeat

THE GOOD FATHER by Maggie Kingsley

Neonatologist Gabriel Dalgleish is passionate about
his tiny patients. It seems as if they are all he cares
for. Except for Maddie. The new medical secretary
slips through Gabriel's defences, right to his
vulnerable heart!

THE BABY DOCTORS
Making families is their business!

On sale 5th May 2006

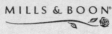

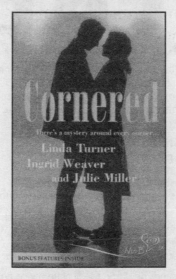

4 FREE

BOOKS AND A SURPRISE GIFT!

We would like to take this opportunity to thank you for reading this Mills & Boon® book by offering you the chance to take FOUR more specially selected titles from the Medical Romance™ series absolutely FREE! We're also making this offer to introduce you to the benefits of the Reader Service™—

- ★ FREE home delivery
- ★ FREE gifts and competitions
- ★ FREE monthly Newsletter
- ★ Exclusive Reader Service offers
- ★ Books available before they're in the shops

Accepting these FREE books and gift places you under no obligation to buy, you may cancel at any time, even after receiving your free shipment. Simply complete your details below and return the entire page to the address below. You don't even need a stamp!

YES! Please send me 4 free Medical Romance books and a surprise gift. I understand that unless you hear from me, I will receive 6 superb new titles every month for just £2.80 each, postage and packing free. I am under no obligation to purchase any books and may cancel my subscription at any time. The free books and gift will be mine to keep in any case.

M6ZED

Ms/Mrs/Miss/Mr ....Initials ....
BLOCK CAPITALS PLEASE

Surname ....

Address ....

....

....Postcode................................

Send this whole page to:
UK: FREEPOST CN81, Croydon, CR9 3WZ